KT-512-027

Alexa Tewkesbury

CWR

Hey!
I'm Rick – I'm in the Dixons Gang.

You might have heard of us. There's me and my mates, Kevin and Clyde, and we all live on the Dixons Estate, in Holly Hill.

There's not that much to do in Holly Hill so we like to hang out together. The best places are the shopping centre and the park – there's lots of room there to play football or ride a bike.

Sometimes we run into the Topz Gang. 'Topzies' we call them just cos it bugs them. They're really annoying – they always seem to be talking about God and I don't get it. Us Dixons, we're cool. But Topz, they're just a waste of space.

I mean, the last thing someone like me needs is them poking about in my business. But there was this one time when I had a secret. Not even Dixons could know.

That's what this story is all about …

Hi! We're the Topz Gang –

Topz because we all live at the 'top' of something …
either in houses at the top of the hill, at the top of the
flats by the park, even sleeping in a top bunk counts!
We are all Christians, and we go to Holly Hill School.
We love Jesus, and try to work out our faith in God
in everything we do – at home, at school and with our
friends. That even means trying to show God's love to
the Dixons Gang who tend to be bullies, and can be a
real pain!

If you'd like to know more about us, visit our website
at **www.cwr.org.uk/topz** You can read all about us,
and how you can get to know and understand the Bible
more by reading our *Topz* notes, which are great fun,
and written every two months just for you!

One

Rick stared down at the envelope in his hands. It had dropped through the letterbox a short while before, landing on the pale blue carpet in the hall. The stamp was a bit crooked and his dad's handwriting was on the front. Rick was sure he knew what was inside, too. A birthday card.

The card's arrival didn't make him happy. The fact that it was his birthday was making him miserable. Exactly a year ago today, Rick's dad had moved away. A long way away.

That was the moment Rick decided he wouldn't 'do' birthdays any more ... he didn't want a reason to remember *that* day.

Something thudded against his bedroom door. He frowned.

'Can we see your card?' a little voice whined from the other side.

'I haven't opened it,' Rick snapped. 'Go away.'

'But we just want to *see* it. Come on, Rick.' Rick's sister, Alesha, banged her shoulder into the door again. Harder this time. Her twin, Naomi, did the same. They were four years old – much younger than Rick but even more stubborn.

'I said, go away!' Rick shouted. 'I haven't opened the stupid card and I'm not going to ... Now, for the last time, leave me *alone*!'

'Naomi! Alesha!' Their mum called up the stairs. She sounded cross. Tired. 'Come down here now. If he's going to be like that, it's best just to come away.'

'But why?' moaned Alesha.

'Because I say so! Get down here and I'll put a DVD on for you.'

Rick heard the two pairs of feet thump moodily down the stairs. He slumped onto his bed. He kept turning the envelope over and over in his hands. No, he wasn't going to open it – no way.

Suddenly, with a flick of his wrist, he threw it. The envelope flew across the room and disappeared behind the chest of drawers in the corner.

Rick flopped backwards onto his duvet. His head bounced on the pillow and he glared up at the ceiling.

It wasn't just that his twin sisters were annoying. Rick could deal with that. He spent a lot of time out of the house with his mates in the Dixons Gang anyway. What really got to him was that the girls had spoiled everything. At least that's how it seemed to him.

Before Naomi and Alesha were born, his parents were together. All right, so his mum and dad didn't always seem like the best of friends, but they still did family stuff with Rick. They went for walks. They went iceskating. They went away for a holiday now and again. As soon as Rick was old enough, his dad had taken him to watch the football on Saturday afternoons. Then they'd have a kickabout with a ball together afterwards. Rick had *loved* those times. They were special. He always thought his dad had loved them, too.

Clearly he hadn't, Rick thought to himself. Otherwise he wouldn't have moved away.

Thud.

Unbelievable. The girls were back. It was probably Alesha who would have been the first to sneak up the stairs again. But Naomi was bound to be there as well.

Where Alesha went, Naomi *had* to follow.

'Ri-ick, have you opened your card yet?'

Rick heard Alesha's singsong voice again and rolled his eyes. He'd had enough. He couldn't stay in the house any longer. It was time to get out. He leapt off the bed, threw his door open, pushed past the twins and raced down the stairs.

'Rick, where's your birthday card?' he heard Naomi wail as he headed for the front door.

'I'm going out, Mum!' he yelled over his shoulder.

The girls didn't have time to catch up with him. By the time they'd reached the door, he'd already slammed it shut after him.

When the other two Dixons found him, Rick was at the shopping centre; slouched on one of the wooden benches opposite the shoe shop.

'What're you doing *here*, Rick?' Clyde demanded. 'We've been waiting for you down the park.'

Neither he nor Kevin wished Rick a happy birthday. They didn't know it *was* his birthday. Rick hadn't told them and they weren't likely to remember from other years.

'I never said I'd be down the park,' Rick muttered.

'Yeah, you did,' said Clyde.

Rick shrugged. 'Don't remember.'

'What's up?' frowned Kevin.

'Nothing.'

'Well, I'm not hanging around here,' grunted Clyde. 'I'm going back to the park. You coming, or what?'

Rick didn't answer.

'Rick?' said Kevin.

'All right, I'm coming,' mumbled Rick. He stood up and jerked his head to flick his fringe out of his eyes. As usual, it instantly flopped back down. The curtain of hair hanging over his forehead was too long, but he refused to have it cut any shorter.

Rick had got cold sitting on the bench. Despite being early April, the start of the Easter holidays, it was a chilly morning. Spring was supposed to be in the air, but it still felt like winter. Rick zipped up his hoodie as he sloped along the pavement. Kevin and Clyde trailed slightly behind.

It was Clyde who spotted Danny and John first. They'd just come out of the corner shop up ahead. They each held a bulging carrier bag. John was bending down to untie the little dog whose lead he'd attached to the newspaper stand.

'Oop-oop-oop!' Clyde wailed, making an alarm – type sound at the top of his voice. 'Danger! Danger! **Topz Gang alert!'**

Danny turned sharply, and John almost toppled over. He accidentally dropped the dog's lead, but it didn't matter. Gruff knew better than to run off when he and John were out in the street.

'Hey, Topzies!' yelled Kevin. 'Hope there's something in those bags for us!'

The Dixons Gang hated Topz. They picked on them whenever they had the chance. As much as they could, Topz kept out of their way. But some days they couldn't help walking right into them – Holly Hill wasn't that big a place.

'Come on, John, let's go,' said Danny quietly.

Most of the time it was better to ignore Dixons. That was what Topz' Sunday Club leader, Greg, said. He kept an eye on the Dixons boys. Sometimes they turned up at youth club on a Friday night. When they did, they were usually just looking to make trouble.

'Don't get in an argument with them if you can help it,' Greg told Topz. 'It's not worth it. If they start something, just walk away. That's the best thing you can do. It's easier said than done, I know, but it's important. There's a way you can help them, too,' he added. 'You can pray for them. See, when kids act the way Dixons do, you can be fairly sure there are reasons for it. What they really need is to know that God cares about them – no matter what.'

As John and Danny tried to head home with their shopping, Clyde ran up, then jumped in front of them. There was a silly grin all over his face.

'Don't you ever go anywhere without your dog, John?' he smirked.

John pulled Gruff's lead in tighter so that the little dog was tucked close to his leg. He and Danny started to walk round Clyde, but Clyde just hopped sideways so that he was blocking their path again.

'What do you want, Clyde?' asked Danny. 'We've got to get back.'

'What's in your shopping?' Clyde demanded.

'Just stuff,' Danny answered.

Kevin stepped forward to stand in front of the Topz boys, too. It made it even harder for them to get past.

'So, don't you, John?' Kevin said.

'Don't I what?' John mumbled, holding Gruff's lead even tighter.

'Don't you ever go anywhere without that stupid

little dog?'

'Hey!' interrupted Rick. 'Don't call the dog stupid, Kevin.' Any other day, Rick would have joined in with Dixons quite happily. Today he wasn't in the mood. 'It's not *his* fault he belongs to a Topz, ' he added.

'I'll call it what I want,' retorted Kevin grimly. He didn't like being told what to do. Especially not in front of Topz boys.

'Then you're the one who's stupid,' Rick grunted. He didn't wait for Kevin to reply, just turned and began to trudge back the way they'd come.

John and Danny grabbed the moment and started to walk away, too. This time, Clyde and Kevin didn't stop them. They couldn't be bothered with Topz now either. Their eyes were still on Rick, who was disappearing back towards the shopping centre.

Ten minutes later, Rick was on the bench opposite the shoe shop again. He wished Dixons hadn't come looking for him. Kevin had put him in an even worse mood.

But then, it wasn't *all* Kevin's fault, Rick had to admit. It was seeing John with his dog.

Today of all days.

John had everything, didn't he?

Perfect family with two perfect parents. Perfect house. Perfect life. And all complete with a perfect little dog of his very own.

Typical Topz.

Rick scowled down at his trainers. His eyes flicked up as a man with a black Labrador walked past. Jogging the other way he spied a girl with a brown and white cocker spaniel trotting at her heels.

There were dogs everywhere. Everyone who wanted one probably had one, Rick thought bitterly.

Except for him. He didn't. Not any more.

They'd had a dog when his dad lived at home. He had black and white short hair and floppy ears. He was a proper 'mixtie', Rick's dad used to say – a mix of different breeds. He had the brightest blue eyes and his tail never stopped wagging. His name was Wolf.

When Rick's dad first left, he had taken Wolf to live with him in his new house in Holly Hill. Now that he'd moved away altogether, Rick hardly ever saw their dog. He didn't see much of his dad either. A year ago today, he felt as if he'd lost both of them forever.

That's why he hated birthdays. That's why he'd always hate them.

Rick scuffed his trainers against the ground. He shivered. He was freezing. He wasn't sure how long he'd been sitting on the bench, but the air still felt as cold as when he'd first left his house. He was getting hungry, too. There was a delicious smell of baking coming from the pasty shop behind him, but he didn't have any money. He'd have to go home.

As he stood up, he watched another dog strolling by with its owner. This one was wearing a special fluorescent harness. Rick's eyes slid from the dog to the lady with it. He saw that she was carrying a white stick. She was blind and her dog was leading her where she needed to go. Keeping her safe.

He remembered what Kevin had said to John: 'Don't you ever go anywhere without that stupid little dog?'

Dogs aren't stupid, he thought to himself, watching the guide dog taking its owner carefully through the busy shopping centre. *It's people who are the stupid ones. Dogs are better than people any day.*

Two

When John and Danny got back to John's house, they stacked the shopping John had bought in a large rucksack. Supplies for his holiday. He was leaving later that day for a camping trip to North Wales with his Uncle Tom and two of his cousins. They were all going to walk up Mount Snowdon. He'd be gone for ten days. If the weather wasn't too bad, they might even stay a fortnight.

By about three o'clock that afternoon, John was all packed and ready to go.

'What time's Dad getting back?' he asked his mum for about the third time since lunch. John's dad was driving him the hour or so's journey to Uncle Tom's house.

'Still around five o'clock,' she said. 'No matter how many times you ask me, John, it's still going to be around five o'clock.'

'But I'm ready to go *now*,' he sighed impatiently.

John wasn't good at waiting. He always got the fidgets. He'd been looking forward to this trip for weeks, and now it made the hanging around even harder.

'If you've got nothing else to do, why don't you take Gruff for another walk?' suggested his mum. 'You might as well. After all, you're not going to see him for a while.'

'Good idea,' John agreed. 'In fact, if Sarah comes with me, I can show her what to do.'

John's twin sister, Sarah, was going to be walking Gruff while John was away. She glanced at him scornfully.

'I think I *know* how to take Gruff for a walk, John,' she said. 'I've been with you loads of times.'

'I know,' he nodded, 'but you've not taken him on your own before.'

'I probably won't *be* on my own. Josie's going to come with me.'

'I know,' John said again. 'But I can show you where Gruff likes to go. We don't always walk to the park, you know. Sometimes we wander round the shopping centre. And we go down through the industrial estate, too. There's that bit of grass there near the new supermarket. Not many people know about it.'

'John, you don't have to show me where to go,' Sarah sighed. 'I live here too, remember! I know where people take their dogs. I'll decide where to walk him when it's time for him to go out.'

'But Gruff needs his routine,' John insisted. 'If I'm not going to be around, it's even more important that he goes where he's used to. Oh, yeah,' he added as another thought struck him, 'and you have to remember to take a bag. To pick up his … you know … his poo.'

'Sarah,' John's mum interrupted, 'go with him, there's a good girl. He's not going to leave you alone until you do.'

Sarah rolled her eyes. 'Fine,' she muttered.

The twins slipped on their trainers. Gruff's lead hung on a hook by the front door. The little dog was already looking interested as John's shoes went on but when John reached up to grab his lead from the hook, he went mad. He darted up and down the hall, pink tongue lolling from his mouth, then began whizzing in circles haphazardly as he chased his tail. Saucy, Sarah's cat, watched sleepily from half way up the stairs.

'You'll get used to this,' said John, trying to catch

hold of Gruff's collar.

'What do you mean, "get used to this"?' Sarah retorted. 'I see Gruff every single day. I *know* what he's like, John.'

'Yes, but you've not had to deal with him before,' John answered. He made another attempt to get hold of Gruff's collar. '*I* know what I'm doing with Gruff. You don't.'

Sarah rolled her eyes again. She reached out and grabbed Gruff's collar just as he was about to make another mad dash across the hall. Holding the little dog still, she snatched the lead away from John with her free hand, then clipped it easily onto the metal loop on the collar.

'You're right, John,' she said, blinking at him, pretending to be deadly serious. 'I don't know how I'm going to manage without you … Shall we go now?'

The three of them headed for the park, Sarah holding on to Gruff's lead. John said they could walk the other way, to the shopping centre, afterwards. There was plenty of time. It was still ages till their dad would be home.

But they hadn't gone far before John was wishing they'd done the walk the other way round.

Dixons were out again. Two of them anyway. Clyde and Kevin were standing on the pavement on the other side of the road, pointing and shouting.

'It's John!' Clyde yelled. 'And look! His sister's got a dog that looks just like his! Well, what d'you know!'

There was a steady stream of cars driving along the road in both directions. It meant there was no way the Dixons boys could get over to their side quickly.

'Don't look at them,' John said to Sarah. 'They were messing about this morning, too.'

'Doing what?' Sarah asked. Both she and John were walking more quickly now.

'Just saying stuff,' John muttered. **'Kevin called Gruff stupid.'**

Sarah frowned. 'That's a horrid thing to say.'

'It's a *Dixons* thing to say.'

That's when they heard the footsteps running up behind them.

'What's this, then?' It was Kevin. 'Have you got *two* stupid dogs in your house now, John?'

John kept his eyes on the pavement. He shook his head. 'This is Gruff,' he said. 'You know it is.'

'Might not be,' Kevin insisted. 'If you're the sort of *stupid* person that likes *stupid* dogs, you might as well have two instead of just one of the stupid things. What sort of a *stupid-looking* dog is that anyway?'

Clyde sniggered.

Sarah could feel herself getting annoyed. Dixons

picked on other kids. They were well known for it. But how dare they pick on Gruff?

'Let's go home, Sarah,' John mumbled. 'I think Gruff's been out long enough.'

He took the dog's lead from her and wound it in tightly. Then he went to pull Sarah with him as he started to walk back the way they'd come.

Sarah didn't budge. She'd been staring down at Kevin's feet. Suddenly her gaze flicked up and she looked him full in the face.

'You haven't got a dog, have you, Kevin?' she said quietly.

'Course not!' scoffed Kevin. 'What would I want one of those *stupid* things for?'

Sarah felt John's hand clamp around her elbow and give her another tug. 'Come on, Sarah, let's go!' he hissed.

But Sarah wasn't moving. Not until she'd finished what she wanted to say. 'If you did have a dog, Kevin,' she went on, 'you'd know that dogs *aren't* stupid. They're actually really clever.'

Turning, she marched off smartly along the pavement. John found himself having to run with Gruff slightly to keep up. Behind them, Kevin and Clyde burst into giggles.

'Ooh!' Clyde shouted after them. 'Scary girly! **You'd better watch yourself**, John! Your sister's  **TERRIFYING!'**

17

Three

'What's the matter now?'

John and Sarah's mum stood in the kitchen doorway, hands planted firmly on her hips. She could hear the twins quarrelling before they'd even stepped inside the front door.

'All I said was take Gruff for a walk together,' she grumbled, 'and you can't even do that without falling out. What's going on?'

John unclipped Gruff's lead and slung it over the hook by the door.

'Sarah's only gone and wound up Dixons,' he moaned. 'I said we should just leave, but she wouldn't listen.'

'I didn't wind them up,' Sarah retorted. 'Kevin was going on about dogs being stupid and I told him they weren't, that's all. What's wrong with that?'

'You shouldn't have said *anything*,' John snapped.

'Well, I wasn't going to stand there and let them call Gruff stupid, was I!'

John shook his head. 'We should have come straight home.'

'We *did* come straight home,' Sarah argued. 'Anyway, they weren't annoyed. They were laughing.'

'That's not the point!' John shouted.

'NO, IT'S NOT!' The twins' mum could shout louder. She'd had plenty of practice. She quite often had to make herself heard over her children's squabbles. 'The point is,' she went on more quietly, as soon as she had their attention, 'you've been out for a walk and you've come back fighting. John, you're about to go on holiday. Sarah, you're not going to see your brother for two weeks. Now, please, will you just be pleasant to each other till your dad gets back.'

There was a pause. 'Sorry, Sarah,' John mumbled. 'Sorry, too,' Sarah answered.

'Right,' their mum sighed. 'Now, John, go and have a look in your room and check you've got everything you're going to need. Sarah, why don't you stay here with me?'

'I can give John a hand,' said Sarah.

John shrugged. 'If you want.'

John's bedroom was looking unnaturally tidy. For once, everything seemed to be where it should be. As he'd packed for his holiday, at the same time he'd stuffed the clothes, books and toys usually scattered over the floor, more or less into their right places.

He checked quickly in his cupboard, but he was fairly sure he hadn't forgotten anything.

Sarah plonked down on his bed. 'If Dixons had called *you* stupid, I'd have stuck up for you, too, you know,' she said.

John gave her a half smile. 'I know,' he replied. 'And I'd have stuck up for you.' He dropped down onto the bed next to her. 'It's just … I don't know why Kevin's so interested in Gruff all of a sudden. And I'm about to go away. You'll be out walking him on your own.'

'I told you, I'll probably be with Josie.'

'I know but *I* won't be there. What if something happens? What if Dixons do something? To Gruff, I mean?'

'Like what?'

'I don't *know*,' John sighed. 'That's the trouble. You never know what Dixons are planning. That's why I got cross. I don't want to give them any more reason to pick on Gruff than they've already got.'

Sarah reached out and gave John's hand a squeeze. 'I'm not going to let anything happen to Gruff,' she said. 'I love him just as much as you do.'

'I know,' John smiled. 'I'm being an idiot.'

'Yeah,' Sarah nodded, 'you are.'

There was the sound of a key in the front door.

'Dad's home,' she said.

John leapt up. His eyes were shining. 'I'm going camping in Wales,' he said, as if he could hardly believe it himself. 'I'm *really* going.'

'Yup,' replied Sarah.

John headed for his bedroom door. When he got there he paused. 'Remember, Gruff can have a handful of biscuits at lunchtime, as well as his breakfast and supper.'

'Yup,' nodded Sarah.

'And Sarah?'

'Yeah?'

'Thanks.'

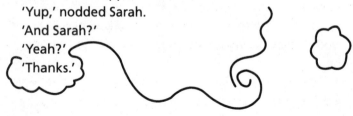

About half an hour after John and his dad had driven off past the shopping centre, a small, white truck trundled along the same road in the opposite direction.

The truck turned right just past the railway station. It ambled on a little further, then the man driving it swung into a narrow street with houses on either side. It was the fourth time today that the driver had made the same journey. It would be the last time today, too. With a jolt, he stopped abruptly outside the first gate on the corner. Number One, Makepiece Avenue.

Number One was a red-brick house on the end of a terrace of similar red-brick houses. The house next door was smart. It had new windows with gleaming white frames. The path from the gate was swept clean and there were pots of daffodils and early tulips by the front door.

Number One, on the other hand, was shabby. It looked even shabbier next to the smartness of its neighbour. There was moss on the roof tiles and on the path. Paint peeled from the old window frames and the front gate dragged on the ground where one of the hinges was broken.

No one had lived there for well over a year. No one ever seemed to go in or out. Rick hadn't seen anyone there for ages.

An alley ran along behind the terrace at the end of the back gardens. Rick nearly always used it as a short cut to the shopping centre and the park. He had got so used to seeing the 'For Sale' board outside Number One when he tramped past that he hardly noticed it any more.

Then one day, a few weeks earlier, it disappeared and a different board was put up instead. This one said, 'Sold'. That's when Rick had got curious. The house had been empty for so long that he couldn't help wondering who would be moving into it now.

After that, whenever he walked through the alley, Rick stopped behind Number One's back garden to check if it was now occupied. A length of wire mesh fixed to thin, metal posts stood in front of a tall, scruffy hedge. They separated the garden from the alley. The hedge wasn't very thick, but it had grown outwards through the holes in the mesh, pushing the fence forwards in places. When Rick crouched down and peered closely, he could see right through into the garden.

The weeks went by, and still there was no one.

Until today.

Rick wasn't there earlier to see the white truck make its first three visits to Makepiece Avenue. He didn't see the driver and the man with him unloading various pieces of furniture into Number One through the broken front gate.

He didn't hear the driver say to his friend, 'Thanks, Ray. I think one more trip should do it. I'll drop you home now, if you like.'

What Rick *did* see as he was about to turn into the alley on his way home, was the white truck drive past him on its fourth visit of the day. He noticed its blinker start to flash. Then, almost as soon as it had driven into the avenue, Rick saw it stop.

A man got out. He was short and a bit tubby, and wore baggy jeans and an old T-shirt. His curly, dark hair had streaks of grey. He went round to the back of the truck and opened it. Reaching inside, he slid out a large, wooden packing case. He grasped it carefully in both arms, then turned towards the gate.

That's when he spotted Rick.

Rick quickly looked away. He went to dive into the alley out of sight, but the man called over: **'You can give me a hand if you want!'**

Rick was startled. 'What?' he called back.

The man smiled. 'You can give me a hand. There's another three of these cases in the back of the truck. I'd be glad of some help.'

For a moment, Rick wasn't sure how to answer. The man seemed friendly enough, but Rick had never seen him before. He knew the safe thing was to say no and get on home.

'I can't,' he mumbled. For some reason, he felt he should make up an excuse so he added, 'It's my birthday and Mum'll be waiting.'

As soon as he'd said it, he wished he hadn't. He hadn't mentioned his birthday to anyone all day. Why was he telling a stranger?

'Oh!' grinned the man. 'Happy birthday! You doing anything nice?'

Rick shook his head. 'Anyway, bye,' he muttered.

The man was still smiling as he headed towards his front door. People were bound to be curious about who was moving in, he knew that. The house had been empty for so long. Several of his new neighbours had already been peering round their curtains. Watching to see who had arrived in the white truck; what sort of people were going to be living at the end of their road.

The man didn't mind. He'd been in a flat for the last few years, which had suited him. It's just that now he really needed a house with a garden. Number One, Makepiece Avenue would do very well.

Four

The day after John had left for his camping trip, the phone rang early in the Topz twins' house. Sarah's mum answered.

'Sarah,' she called. 'John wants to speak to you.'

Sarah took the phone, looking puzzled.

'John,' she said, 'it's eight o'clock in the morning. Why are you ringing so early? You can't have got lost already.'

'No,' John replied cheerfully. 'We're still at Uncle Tom's house. We've just had breakfast. That's why I thought I'd ring.'

'Because you've just had breakfast?' frowned Sarah.

'No,' said John. 'Because having breakfast reminded me that it must be time for Gruff to have *his* breakfast.'

'Yes,' Sarah nodded, 'he's just had it.'

'Well, I just thought I'd check that he'd eaten it all right. If dogs are sad, they can sometimes go off their food. I read it on the Internet.'

Sarah said nothing.

'So did he eat breakfast all right?'

'He ate loads of breakfast, John,' Sarah replied, as patiently as she could. 'I'm sure he's not sad. He looks just like he always does. Anyway, I've got to go. Josie's coming round in a minute so we can take him out. Hope you find the mountain. Bye.'

By the time Josie rang the front door bell, Sarah was already wearing her trainers and had clipped Gruff's lead onto his collar.

It was early on a Saturday. The road to the park was still quite busy with cars, but quieter than a weekday morning. Gruff trotted along happily between the two girls.

'Do you suppose he wonders where John is?' Josie asked.

'Probably,' Sarah replied. 'He seems all right, though. And I tell you what,' she added with a grin, 'it's great being able to get into the bathroom whenever I want to. And the smell of socks has gone already!'

Josie giggled.

Then she suddenly stopped still on the pavement.

'Uh-oh,' she muttered, nodding towards a figure up ahead. 'Clyde.'

Sarah followed Josie's gaze. Leaning against a lamppost by the park entrance was a boy with a thick mop of ginger hair. He looked bored and was using one hand to bounce a football up and down.

'Bother,' sighed Sarah. 'Oh, well. Let's keep walking. He probably won't take any notice of us if he's on his own.'

A moment later, there was a shout.

'Clyde! Over here!' It was Kevin, with Rick at his heels. The two of them were already in the park. They'd spotted the third Dixon at the same time as the girls.

Clyde made for the park gate, then stopped. He threw the ball into the air and, with a well-aimed kick, sent it flying towards them. Rick headed it right back. Pleased with himself, he punched the air enthusiastically. Then the three of them ran off, shouting and laughing, kicking the football between them as they went.

Sarah and Josie took a few steps nearer to the park entrance. They stood looking after Dixons as they raced off. Gruff was getting impatient and starting to pull on his lead.

'They're going right up the other end,' said Josie. 'They'll never see us from over there. We can just stay around here.'

Keeping to the edge of the park near the gates, the girls wandered around with Gruff snuffling about in the grass in front of them. They didn't let him off the lead. They wanted to keep him close.

They were so busy chatting that they almost forgot Dixons.

Until Sarah had a funny feeling. The sort of feeling that creeps over you unexpectedly.

The feeling that they were being watched.

Turning her head sharply, she saw Rick standing nearby, staring. He was on his own this time

on the path a little way away from them. There was no sign of the other two. They must still have been playing football.

But Rick's expression surprised Sarah. He wasn't scowling the way he often did. His face was quite blank, she thought. He wasn't even looking at her and Josie. His eyes were fixed on Gruff.

Instinctively, Sarah pulled Gruff's lead in tighter. Josie had seen Rick now, too. She took a step closer to her friend. The pair of them waited.

What would Rick say? What would he *do*?

But nothing happened. Nothing was said. After a few moments, Rick dropped his gaze and slunk off out of the park.

The girls didn't hang around to see if the other two Dixons boys would be following. They gave Rick a moment to get out of their way, then they headed for home.

Rick couldn't stay out long. The mobile hairdresser was coming round to his house that morning and his mum had sent him to buy biscuits.

'You can do the lot of us while you're here, Denise,' his mum had said when she'd made the appointment. 'I'll get some Custard Creams in and we'll have a good natter.'

Rick's mum loved having her hair cut. She always had the full wash, cut and blow dry. 'It's a little bit of time just for me,' she'd say. 'And let's face it, I get precious little of *that*.'

It was Rick's job to keep an eye on his twin sisters

while his mum had her 'me time'. Things didn't always go to plan. Some squabble or other would usually break out. Then Rick's mum would be forced to leap out of her chair shouting, 'What is going *on*? Can't I even have five minutes to myself? Rick! What are you doing, you're supposed to be helping me here!'

Naomi and Alesha liked it when Denise came. The twins were both brown-eyed, with shiny brown hair to match. Denise always trimmed it to shoulder length with a pair of sharp, red-handled scissors. Then she tidied up their thick, floppy fringes to just above their eyebrows.

Rick, on the other hand, hated having his hair messed with by anyone. He'd already decided that when he was old enough *not* to be told what to do any more, he'd never have it cut again. He'd just let it grow and grow, and wear it in a long ponytail down his back.

On his way home from playing football in the park, Rick stopped at the corner shop to buy the Custard Cream biscuits. Then he turned off the main road and ambled towards the Dixons Estate. He wasn't in any hurry. A haircut was nothing to rush back for. His mum would get in a bad mood with him if he was late to look after the twins. But then she'd probably be in a bad mood with him anyway. She usually was. Nothing he did was right. She'd been angry almost every day since his dad had left. In any case, she seemed to think more of her two girls than she'd ever thought of him.

It wasn't until Rick reached the alley behind Makepiece Avenue that he suddenly remembered the newcomer. The man with the curly hair who had moved into Number One the day before. Rick wondered if he'd see him again today; if the man would remember him as the boy with the birthday.

He peeped round to the front of the house before stepping into the alley. There was no sign of anyone. The gate seemed to have given up, though. Being opened and closed so many times yesterday on only one hinge had clearly been too much for it. It lay flat on the ground next to the path.

As he turned into the alley, Rick stumbled. He almost dropped the biscuits. Glancing down, he saw that one of his shoelaces had come undone. He tucked the biscuits under one arm and crouched to tie it up again.

That's when he noticed it. An odd sort of sound. It was quite soft but Rick still heard it straight away. Something was snuffling along the bottom of the hedge at the end of Number One's garden.

Rick kept still, listening. After a moment, he slowly leaned forwards and peered through the straggle of dark green leaves and twigs pushing out through the wire fence. At first he couldn't make anything out. Just grass that badly needed cutting stretching away towards the house.

Then suddenly there was something there! A dark shape appeared in front of him on the other side of the hedge.

Neither Rick nor the shape moved. The snuffling from the garden stopped, too. Rick held his breath.

Then, almost at once, the funny sound began again.

Pushing his face as close to the wire mesh as he could without getting scratched, Rick screwed up his eyes in an effort to see what it was in the garden.

It was then that the dark shape gave itself away. It barked.

The sound was really more like a hiccup than a bark, but it was enough to make Rick jump. He lost his balance and toppled over backwards. The biscuits under his arm slipped to the ground. Rick left them where they were. He was much more interested in getting a proper look at the dog that now seemed to live at Number One, Makepiece Avenue.

Five

'Where have you been?' Rick's mum snapped at him the moment he stepped inside the front door. 'Denise did the twins' hair ages ago. "Don't worry," I said to her, "Rick'll be home before you get on to mine." But were you home, Rick? No, you weren't. She still managed to cut mine, bless her, although I don't know how. Not with the number of times I had to get up and sort the girls out because you *weren't here* to keep an eye on them.' Her voice got louder. '*And* we couldn't even have a biscuit with our coffee while we waited for you to get back so she could cut yours!'

Rick handed her the packet of Custard Creams. 'Sorry,' he muttered. 'You can have one now.'

'Now?' his mum said crossly. 'It's too late now, Rick! Denise has gone.'

'I'm sorry,' Rick mumbled again.

'I don't know what gets into you,' his mum grumbled on. 'You give me no help. No support. It's not easy with the twins, you know. Sometimes I don't know why I keep bothering with any of you.'

'Then *don't* keep bothering,' Rick answered moodily. **'Dad doesn't.'**

Rick's mum looked at him miserably for a moment. Then, 'Where have you been anyway?' she asked. 'I only wanted you to go and buy some biscuits.'

Rick nodded. 'And I bought them,' he retorted. 'I'll be upstairs.'

'But where have you been?' Rick's mum watched him plod up to his bedroom. She knew it was hard for him now that his dad had moved away. It was hard for her, too. But he wouldn't talk to her about it and she didn't know what to say to him. So they always ended up saying nothing.

At that moment, all Rick wanted to do was think about the dog he'd just met.

He knew you should never put your hand out to a dog you didn't know. Especially if the dog was on its home ground. In its own garden. He remembered his dad telling him that often enough. Sticking his fingers through the fence at the end of Number One, Makepiece Avenue's garden would normally have been a very silly thing to do.

But it was weird. As much as Rick wanted to get up close to the dog to say hello properly, he had the strong feeling that the dog wanted to say hello to him, too. So much so, that the animal had pushed his black head as far through the tangle of leaves and twigs as he could, until his nose almost touched the wire fence.

Rick held the back of one hand against the mesh and let the dog have a good sniff. His soft, brown eyes seemed to search the boy's face. Slowly, so as not to frighten him, Rick inched forwards. Then, very carefully, he reached behind the wire mesh. Straight away, the dog tried to push his head upwards to meet Rick's hand. There was too much hedge in the way for him to move far, but Rick was able to stretch down and scratch the dog's pointed ears with his fingers. All the time, he watched the animal's face. He was ready to pull back quickly if he saw any sign that he wanted to be left alone.

But to Rick's delight, the dog seemed more than happy to be getting some attention.

'What's your name, then?' he asked softly. 'I had a dog once, you know. He was called Wolf. Be funny if your name was Wolf, too. He was black like you. But his eyes were blue, and he had white patches and his ears were floppy. I don't think there's any white on you, is there?'

Rick peered through the hedge. He could just about make out the rest of the dog's body. He had a red collar round his neck and for a moment, it did look as if he was black all over. Then he shifted his position slightly, which is when Rick spotted it. The dog had one perfectly white back foot.

'Ha!' Rick laughed. 'Look at that!'

'Look at what? What are you doing?'

Rick was so startled at the voice that he snapped upright, dragging his arm from between the fence and the hedge. His hand caught on a piece of wire where the mesh was broken. It dug a bright red scratch into his palm.

Rick wasn't the only one who was startled. The dog instantly shot back through the hedge and disappeared.

At the entrance to the alleyway stood Clyde.

'Clyde!' Rick hissed. 'What are you sneaking up on me for?'

'I'm not sneaking up on you,' Clyde retorted. 'I'm on my way home.'

'Well, you've scared him away now.'

Clyde shook his head. 'Scared who away?'

'The dog!'

'What dog?'

'The one in the garden!' Rick snapped.

He wanted to shout at Clyde. But at the same time, he didn't want to scare the dog even more. And he certainly didn't want the man who'd just moved into the house to know he was there.

Clyde was looking at him as if he'd gone mad. 'OK,' he shrugged. 'There's a dog in the garden. So what?'

Rick bent down and grabbed the biscuits he'd dropped. 'I was talking to him, that's what,' he muttered.

There was silence for a moment, then Clyde burst out laughing. 'You were *talking* to a dog?' he spluttered.

'Yes. And ...? What's so funny?' Rick demanded.

'Are you going soft?'

Rick couldn't be bothered with this any more. 'I'm off home,' he snarled. Clyde could be so annoying sometimes.

As he stormed off down the alley, the ginger-haired boy was still standing there, staring after him.

Smirking all over his face.

When Rick got upstairs having safely missed his haircut, he remembered his hand. He held it up and inspected the palm. The scratch wasn't that deep, but it was long and felt sore when he opened and closed his fingers. He went to the bathroom, turned on the cold tap at the basin, and let the water run over it. It stung and he pulled a face. He peered down at the cut, but it was something else that caught his eye. His mouth lifted into a smile.

Clinging to the sleeve of his green hoodie was a short, wiry, black hair.

After lunch, Rick went out again. The dog wouldn't still be in the garden, he was sure of it. He'd probably be out walking with his owner. It was sunny. Still not warm exactly, but just right for dog-walking. Rick decided he'd head for the park. If they were there, he'd be sure to spot them. He wondered if the dog would recognise him from this morning.

Rick cut through the alley behind the avenue, the way he always did. He barely slowed at the end to glance through the hedge at Number One.

But his eye was caught by a sudden movement. There was the rustle of twigs and leaves. The dog must have had his head pushed through to the wire mesh again. Rick's arrival had obviously spooked him and he'd jerked backwards into the garden.

Rick stopped instantly. He hunched down, put his hands against the fence and peered hard. The dog was still standing there. He hadn't run away into the house. Rick could just make him out on the other side of the hedge.

Quietly, calmly, so as not to scare him again, Rick called out. **'Hey, dog. Come here. Come on, come over here. Good boy.'**

To begin with, the dog didn't move, but Rick wouldn't give up. He kept on calling, soft and low. 'Here, boy. Come on, let's say hello again.'

At last, ears pricked and black nose twitching, the dog thrust his head back through the tangle of hedge towards the fence. Rick stretched an arm down and stroked the sleek, black hair between his ears. It felt cold.

'What are you doing still out in the garden?' he asked. 'Maybe you've been out for a walk, have you? It's a good day for a walk. I thought you might be in the park right now.'

As much as he could manage under the hedge, the dog kept shoving his head upwards into the Dixons boy's hand.

After a moment, Rick heard voices. They weren't coming from the garden, but from round the corner on the avenue. The dog heard them, too. In a second he'd vanished. He shuffled backwards through the hedge and shot across the grass. Rick couldn't see him any more, but he knew why. He recognised one of the voices. It belonged to the man who'd just moved into Number One. It still sounded friendly and cheerful. Just the way it had when the man had spoken to Rick yesterday.

Now they'll be going for a walk, he thought.

'I haven't moved far,' the man was saying, probably to a neighbour. 'Just needed somewhere a bit bigger, that's all.'

'Plenty to do in that house, though,' said the other voice. It was a lady. 'I doubt it's seen a lick of paint for years.'

'You're right there,' the man replied. 'As a matter of fact, I was just off out to buy some new paintbrushes. I thought I'd do a spot of decorating before I get properly unpacked.'

'Well, I won't hold you up,' said the lady. 'I'm Pat, by the way.'

'Nice to meet you, Pat,' replied the man. 'And I'm Graham. Graham Collins.'

The voices stopped. Rick stood against the back wall of the alley. In a minute, Graham would come back through the house. That's what Rick was waiting for. He wanted to hear Graham call his dog. He wanted to hear the dog's name. Even if Graham was only going shopping, he'd take his dog, too, wouldn't he? Of course he would. Rick's dad took their Wolf everywhere. Even to work with him.

The next sound Rick heard was a door slamming. But it wasn't a house door. It belonged to a car. Then there was the noise of an engine starting up. Still keeping back against the wall, Rick moved towards the alley entrance. A moment later, a small, dark blue car chugged past. Graham was driving – and Rick was sure there was no dog on the back seat.

As soon as the car was out of sight, Rick stepped close to the hedge again. Graham hadn't even put his dog into the house before he left. Rick could hear him a short way away. He was whining.

'Hey, dog!' he called over. 'I'm still here. You're not on your own.'

The whining stopped almost straight away and suddenly, there the dog was, pushing his head towards Rick again. Rick fondled his ears.

'It's all right, you know – whatever your name is,' he said. 'I'll keep you company.'

But it wasn't all right. Rick knew it was all wrong. No wonder the dog's hair felt cold. He was shut out in the garden. Supposing he'd been left outside all day?

Six

Next morning, Rick was out early. His mum needed a few things from the corner shop, but it was raining and both the twins seemed to be coming down with colds.

'I don't want to take them out in this, Rick,' his mum said. 'Either you can stay at home with them, or I'll give you a list and you can get the shopping for me.'

Rick wasn't happy. It was always 'do this', 'do that' through the holidays. Not much of a holiday at all. But if he went and got the shopping, at least he'd be able to check on the dog at Number One on his way.

'Please don't be long this time,' his mum added, pushing a carrier bag and her purse into his hands. 'You can go out again afterwards, if you want to. Not that I know why you would on a day like this.'

Rick stuffed the bag and purse into his pocket. Then he set off, walking quickly, pulling his hood up as he went. He'd almost reached Makepiece Avenue, when he found himself catching up with two other boys also walking along the pavement. They, too, had their hoods pulled well up over their heads.

Rick crept up behind them, grabbed a hood in each hand, and wrenched them down.

'Oi!' the boys shouted out, twisting round.

When he saw Rick standing there grinning, Kevin groaned, 'Oh, I might have known!'

'Yeah, thanks for that, Rick,' added Clyde, trying to pull his hood back up over his mass of hair. 'Now I've got rain down my neck.'

'Where are you going anyway?' asked Kevin.

'Shop,' Rick answered. 'You?'

'Same,' said Kevin.

By now, they'd turned and were walking along the alley. Nearly at the end, Rick stopped.

'OK,' he said. 'See you later, then.'

'I thought you were going to the shop,' replied Kevin.

'Yeah, I am,' nodded Rick. 'But I've got something to do first.'

'Oh, yeah?' said Clyde. 'What's that, then?'

'Nothing,' Rick shrugged. 'Nothing to do with you anyway.'

'What do you mean by that?' Kevin demanded.

'Nothing, all right?' Rick said again.

But Clyde had already realised where they were – standing near the garden where he'd surprised Rick yesterday. The garden where Rick had seen a dog.

'I know what it is!' he smirked. 'Rick's made friends with an invisible dog, haven't you, Rick? He just wants to have another little chat. That's it, isn't it?'

Rick could feel his teeth clenching together.

'What are you on about?' Kevin frowned.

Clyde opened his mouth ready to make some other stupid comment, but Rick stopped him.

'He's not an invisible dog,' he snapped. 'He's real. I just want to check he's OK. Is that all right with you, Clyde?' he finished, with a snarl in his voice.

Clyde held his hands up and shook his head. 'Hey, nothing to do with me.'

'So, where is this dog?' Kevin asked.

Rick looked past him towards the hedge behind the last garden along the alley.

'He's right there,' he said quietly.

And there the dog was; nose pressed close to the wire mesh fence; ears pricked; brown eyes, large and curious.

Rick had spotted him pushing his way through the hedge a moment before.

He took a step forwards. The dog didn't run away. He just carried on watching the boy in front of him. As Rick reached down to stroke his head, he nuzzled an ear into the outstretched hand. The hair on his head felt damp under Rick's fingers. Oily.

'OK, the dog's real,' grunted Clyde. 'So what?'

'*So what?*' hissed Rick, angry but still keeping his voice down. 'Look at him! He's soaking wet. I'm sure he was outside all day yesterday, and now he's been left out in the rain. You can't do that to a dog.'

'Nothing to do with us, is it?' Kevin said.

'Of course it's to do with us,' retorted Rick. 'We know he's here, don't we?'

'Told him yesterday he'd gone soft,' mumbled Clyde to Kevin. 'Anyway, dog's not the only one that's wet. I'm getting cold standing here. Can we just get to the shop?'

'Yeah, let's go,' answered Kevin. He looked at Rick. 'Are you coming, or what?'

Rick stared at the pair of them in disbelief. 'Don't you even care?'

'Like I said,' Kevin shrugged, 'it's got nothing to do with us.'

He and Clyde took the last few steps to the end of the alley and disappeared round the corner.

'It's all right,' Rick murmured, still stroking the dog's damp head. 'You don't need them. They don't know anything. Nothing about dogs anyway. But I do,' he whispered, leaning his forehead against the wire mesh. 'I know you don't like being left on your own. Not for hours on end. Our Wolf never got left on his own like this. My dad knew it would have made him sad.

He knew he wanted company. My dad's good with dogs, you see. He knows what they need … Trouble is, he's gone …'

Rick's voice trailed off. Suddenly, somewhere deep inside his head, he could see himself with his dad again. They were charging around in the park together, kicking a ball. Rick was a much smaller boy then. He looked much happier, too. Happier than he remembered feeling in ages. Joining in the game was a lively, black and white dog. He was chasing the ball with them; nudging it with his nose; leaping backwards and forwards. 'Ricky!' his dad shouted. 'Kick it to me!' The much smaller Rick did. The ball flew. 'Superb kick, Ricky boy! Superb!' his dad crowed …

Something cold and wet thrust itself into Rick's hand. The picture in his mind faded. Rick was glad. He hated thinking about his dad. He did everything he could not to. It's just that sometimes … he couldn't help it.

He looked down. The dog in the garden of Number One, Makepiece Avenue was gazing up at him. He'd lifted his head so that his nose rested against Rick's palm.

'Maybe I should go and knock on Graham what's-his-name's door,' Rick said slowly, more to himself than to the dog. 'Then I can tell him what dogs need. Maybe he doesn't know. Yes,' he nodded, 'yes, that's what I'll do. I'll go and talk to Graham. He spoke to me before. I'm sure he'll speak to me again. I'll just tell him you can't leave a dog on its own like this. It's not fair. I'll go and tell him now.'

Rick pulled his hand out from behind the fence. The dog followed him with his eyes. His deep brown gaze never once left the Dixons boy's face.

'It's all right dog, I'll be straight back,' Rick said, as

reassuringly as he could. 'I'm just going to see Graham. I won't be a minute'

He ran out of the alley.

There were no garages attached to the houses in Makepiece Avenue. The people who lived there parked their cars in the road. Both sides were almost completely full. There was just the odd space next to the pavements that ran up and down the street.

Rick noticed the gap on the end immediately. The one outside Number One. The blue car he'd seen Graham drive away in yesterday was nowhere to be seen. Neither was the white truck Graham had used to move all his stuff into his new house. Rick was disappointed. He must be out, unless he'd left his car somewhere else. Rick decided to ring the doorbell just in case.

He pressed the button. It set off a faint chiming sound inside the house. He waited. His glance fell on the front gate that had fallen off its hinges and still lay on the ground. In the house, nothing moved.

'He's out, dear,' a lady's voice said. She was standing on the pavement looking at him. She carried a shopping bag in one hand and was huddled under a red umbrella. 'Gone to work.'

As Rick looked at her, he wondered whether this was the lady whose voice he'd heard yesterday.

'Gone to *work?*' he replied. He couldn't keep the surprise out of his voice. It made it even more difficult to understand why Graham would have left his dog in the garden. Out in the rain. 'Do you know how long for?'

The lady shook her head. 'No idea. I only saw him for a moment.'

'Do you know where he works, then?'

'The hospital,' the lady answered. 'He does shift

work apparently. He's a porter there, or something like that. Nice man,' she added, and continued on her way.

Rick shook his head. No, he thought. Graham wasn't a 'nice' man. He'd left his dog all on his own. He'd as good as abandoned him! People who abandoned the ones who needed them – the ones they were supposed to love – weren't 'nice'.

Seeing the lady with her shopping bag reminded Rick that he was meant to be going to the shop for his mum. He didn't want to. He didn't want to leave the dog. On the other hand, the quicker he went, the quicker he could get back. He might find some cheap dog biscuits, too. Just something he could bring with him as a treat.

Rick ran round to the alley. The dog was right where he'd left him. Nose at the fence.

'I'm going to get you something,' he smiled. 'Something you'll like.' He gazed deep into the dog's eyes, willing him to understand. 'And I'm going to make sure you're all right. Good boy. I won't be long.'

He shot off at a run. His head and shoulders felt soggy and uncomfortable. The rain had soaked right into his hoodie. He didn't care. All he was interested in was getting back to Makepiece Avenue.

He raced along the streets towards the corner shop in Holly Hill. As it came into view, he reached into his pocket and pulled out his mum's purse. The shopping list she'd given him was inside. He unfolded it and gave it a quick glance. There wasn't much written on it. It shouldn't take long to grab those few things.

It was when Rick looked up again that he saw Gruff. He was sitting by the newspaper stand outside the shop. Rick didn't realise straight away that it *was* Gruff. It was just a small, browny-coloured dog. But then he saw Sarah standing there, looking in through the shop window as she held his lead.

Rick stopped running for a moment. Topz were like Dixons, he thought. It seemed that everywhere you went, you couldn't help bumping into them. But for once, he didn't mind.

'Hey! Sarah!' Rick called, beginning to march smartly towards her.

Sarah spun round. Her eyes widened when she saw the long-haired, lanky Dixons boy. 'Oh, no!' she groaned quietly. 'That's all we need, Gruff.'

She turned back anxiously to the shop window. Josie was inside somewhere but there was no sign of her.

When Sarah looked round again, she and the Dixons boy were almost nose to nose.

Seven

'What?' Rick demanded.

Sarah's eyes narrowed slightly. 'What do you mean?' she answered nervously.

'What's wrong?' Rick asked. 'You look scared to bits. What do you think I'm going to do – eat your hair, or something?'

'I don't know,' Sarah shrugged, trying as hard as she could to put some sort of face on that wouldn't give away how she was really feeling. 'But I'm not scared.'

Her eyes flicked towards the shop doorway. *Come on, Josie*, she thought, *how long does it take to buy a bottle of milk?*

Rick looked down at Gruff. The little dog had stood up as the Dixons boy came towards them. He was watching Rick carefully, and he wasn't wagging his tail. Sarah followed Rick's gaze, and pulled Gruff a little closer.

'So why are *you* taking the dog out?' Rick wanted to know. 'Where's John?'

'He's away,' Sarah replied, as casually as she could. 'He's gone camping. He rings every day, though. Usually more than once. He likes to check that Gruff's all right. You know, that there aren't any ... *problems*.'

As she said the word 'problems', Sarah forced herself to look Rick right in the eye.

He frowned. 'What sort of problems?'

'I don't know,' Sarah said. 'He just likes to check, that's all.'

To her surprise, Rick didn't come back with some smart comment, the way she was expecting him to.

He wasn't even looking at her in that scornful way Dixons usually looked at Topz.

Instead, he nodded his head thoughtfully. 'That's nice of him,' he said. 'Shows he cares.' He glanced down at Gruff again. 'Can I stroke him?'

This time, Sarah was so surprised that for a moment she couldn't speak.

'Can I stroke him?' she heard Rick say again.

'Erm ... OK,' she managed.

Rick crouched down and put out his hand slowly. Gruff backed away a little. He knew Dixons. He knew that whenever he and John ran into them when they were out for a walk, John didn't like it. He knew that Sarah was nervous now.

'It's all right, Gruff,' Sarah gulped. 'It's fine. This is Ricky.'

Rick shot her a look. 'It's *Rick*,' he said firmly. 'No one calls me Ricky. Not any more. I don't like it.'

'Sorry,' Sarah mumbled. She bent down, too, and began to scratch Gruff behind one of his ears to reassure him.

Rick stretched out his fingers and scratched behind the other one. Gruff was clearly uncertain, but after a moment or two, he sat back down. Fuss was still fuss after all, and he loved it.

'I wanted to ask you something,' Rick said suddenly. 'Because you know about dogs.'

'Yeah?' Sarah answered. This meeting was getting odder and odder.

'I mean, *I* know about them, too,' Rick went on. 'They need company, don't they? They like being around you. Joining in with things.'

Sarah nodded.

'You don't ever leave Gruff on his own all day, do

you?' he asked.

'Of course not,' Sarah said. 'He'd be miserable if we did that.'

'Exactly!' agreed Rick. 'It'd make him miserable so you wouldn't do it.'

Sarah was watching him closely. Five minutes ago, she'd never have believed Rick would talk to her like this. Or to any of Topz.

And he seemed sad, she thought. There was something lonely in his face; an empty look in his eyes. He didn't always look like that, did he? If he did, she'd never noticed it before.

'So anyway,' Rick went on, 'if you were going to buy Gruff a treat, what would you get? You know, something nice to eat. I mean, you wouldn't want to end up getting the wrong thing, would you? Might upset his tummy.'

This was so weird! Almost *too* weird! Maybe it wasn't real. Maybe Josie had been in the shop for so long that Sarah had fallen asleep and was having the weirdest of weird dreams!

'Well ...' she began slowly. Even in a dream you answered people when they spoke to you. 'Mostly Gruff has biscuits as a treat, if he's been really good or something. But sometimes we buy chew sticks as well. They've got them in the shop here.'

Rick was smoothing the rough hair on top of Gruff's head with the palm of his hand. 'Would you show me?' he said.

Before Sarah could answer, Josie bounced out of the shop doorway. In one hand she held a plastic bottle of milk, and in the other, an enormous bar of fruit and nut chocolate. The chocolate looked real enough. Perhaps it wasn't a dream after all.

Josie spotted Rick instantly. She stopped abruptly and sucked in her breath. 'You all right, Sarah?' she gulped.

'I'm fine,' Sarah nodded. 'Look, could you just stay with Gruff a minute? Rick wants me to help him find something in the shop.'

Josie's mouth dropped wide open. Sarah didn't say anything else. She just handed Gruff's lead to her startled friend, then disappeared into the corner shop with Rick right behind her.

All the way home, Sarah couldn't stop talking. She told Josie everything Rick had said. She tried to explain the way he'd looked at her; how he'd stroked Gruff so kindly; how he'd shown that he could be … *nice*.

'I mean, whoever thought a Dixon could *be* like that?' she gabbled. 'Especially Rick! He obviously really loves dogs. He says they used to have one and I might remember seeing them all out together. But I don't. Do you, Josie? I asked what happened to their dog, but he wouldn't talk about it. And I thought they might be getting another one. I thought that must be why he was so interested to know about Gruff. But he said, no, he wasn't, and then he got a bit funny with me. He didn't seem to want to talk about that either. But, can you believe it, Josie? Can you believe he spoke to me like that? So … *nicely*? It was amazing! I mean, I am totally and utterly **GOBSMACKED!** Wait till I tell John!'

Sarah couldn't wait to talk to God about it either.

God, the most amazing, weird thing happened today. Rick talked to me! He **actually** *talked to me! He wasn't rude or horrible or mean. He asked me things and he listened to what I said. I thought I was dreaming, but I wasn't. It really happened. And it's all because of Gruff. Rick wanted to know all about him. How many walks a day he has; what he likes to eat; whether he has any toys to play with. He says he's not getting a dog, but I think he must be. Otherwise I don't know why he'd have wanted to know all that stuff.*

But, God, there was something really sad about Rick, too. It was odd. He was saying how dogs should be looked after properly. How they shouldn't be left on their own to get unhappy and lonely. How they need people to love them. But there was this thing in the way he looked, God. Something in the way he spoke to me. I couldn't help feeling that Rick was the one who was unhappy and lonely. It was almost as if he was talking about himself.

I don't know much about him, God, but I remember we were talking about Dixons once with Greg at Sunday Club. They'd been really mean. Paul and Benny had gone to the park to play football the day before. They'd left their bikes by the fence and Dixons had gone and stuck drawing pins in their tyres. Paul was really upset and Benny was mad as anything. But Greg said we should pray for Dixons. Well, that was the last thing we felt like doing but Greg said that there might be things going on we didn't know about, reasons why they were acting this way. He said he knew that Rick's dad had just moved away and Rick was probably feeling quite confused. Rejected even. Greg said that if Rick did feel like that, it might make him do horrible things. He might want to hurt someone else because of the way he'd been hurt.

So we did pray, do you remember, God? We prayed for them right there in Sunday Club. And Benny was amazing because, even though he'd been so cross, he still asked You to be really close to Rick and show him that You love him even if he feels like his own dad doesn't. Benny even said sorry to You for being angry about what Dixons had done to the bikes. It seems like ages ago now, but I won't forget it.

And now this has happened. When Rick came up to me, I thought he was going to say something nasty about Gruff, but he didn't. He **stroked** him! It was as if he wanted to make friends with him.

So I'm wondering, God, if this means there'll be a way for me to get to know Rick more. I could tell him that of course he can be friends with Gruff if he wants to be. Maybe I could even talk to him about You. Like Benny said, I could tell him that You love him even if he feels like his own dad doesn't. He needs You so much, God. There was something about him today that seemed so lonely. He's part of the Dixons Gang, but he still seemed so ... lonely.

Please help me find a way to talk to him about You, God. Please help me to help him.

When Rick got home with the shopping, his mum wasn't happy.

'What did I say before you went out?' she said. '*Please don't be long.*'

'I *haven't* been long,' Rick grunted.

'You've been over an hour, Rick. It doesn't take over an hour to go to the corner shop for a few bits of shopping.'

'I'm sorry,' he muttered. 'I wasn't watching the time.'

His mum shook her head. 'No, that's the trouble. You never watch the time, do you?'

Naomi appeared in the kitchen doorway. 'Mummy?' she said. Her cold was getting worse. She sounded snuffly and she was dabbing at her nose with a tissue. 'The DVD's finished. Can we watch another one?'

'Of course you can,' her mum answered. 'And Mummy'll bring you another drink in a minute.' She glanced at Rick. 'Rick, go and change the DVD for them, would you? I'll just put the shopping away.'

Naomi shuffled back to the lounge, still nursing her nose. She thought Rick was right behind her.

He wasn't. He'd stopped just outside the kitchen and turned back to his mum.

'Mum,' he said. 'Can we get another dog?'

His mum was putting a sliced loaf into the bread bin. 'Another dog? What do we want another dog for?' she replied, opening a cupboard door and sliding two tins of baked beans onto a shelf.

'I loved it when Wolf was here,' Rick said. 'I really miss having a dog.'

His mum peered at him. 'And just who's going to walk this dog, if we get another one?' she asked.

'Me. I will.'

'Hmm. You say that now, but I know exactly what would happen,' his mum retorted. 'The minute it's cold or it's wet or you want a lie-in or you'd rather be with your mates in the park – then it'd be down to me, wouldn't it?'

Rick shook his head. 'No,' he said firmly. 'If I say I'll walk it, I'll walk it.'

'Of course you won't,' his mum went on. She put the last of the shopping in the fridge, then folded up the carrier bag. 'So, no, Rick, I'm sorry but we're not getting another dog. End of story.'

Rick frowned at her. 'But I know this dog that's really unhappy. I don't think he's being looked after properly. He needs someone. I could take care of him.'

'No,' Rick's mum sighed, closing her eyes tiredly. 'How many times do I have to say it? Honestly, Rick, don't you think I've got enough to do?'

'Ri-ick?' Naomi was standing behind him. 'Rick, you're supposed to be doing the DVD.'

'Do it yourself!' he snapped, then he spun round and brushed past her. A moment later, he'd slammed the front door.

Eight

When Rick's dad rang a few days later, Rick wasn't at home. He was hunched in the alley fussing over the dog in the garden at Number One. He'd started taking him biscuits. Today he'd given him a chew stick. Sarah had shown him where to find the ones they bought for Gruff in the corner shop. As usual the dog was by himself. Graham's dark blue car wasn't parked on the avenue because he was at work.

Rick's dad owned a small workshop tucked away in a corner of an industrial estate a short way from Rick's house. He was a mechanic and that's where he used to tinker with all sorts of different engines before he moved away.

He was brilliant with them. Broken-down cars, motorbikes, lawnmowers, boats – whatever the problem, Rick's dad always found a way to solve it. He used to take Rick to work with him sometimes, along with Wolf. Rick would perch on an oily stool, watching his dad take things apart, clean them, tighten up the nuts and bolts and put everything back together. Wolf would watch, too. He was a clever dog. He knew exactly where he was allowed to sit in the workshop to keep safe. He never went where he wasn't supposed to.

When he moved away, Rick's dad didn't sell the workshop. A friend of his rented it from him. But the friend had moved on as well, and now the workshop was empty again. The key had been dropped off with Rick's mum who was keeping it until Rick's dad could visit and pick it up.

But he hadn't been able to visit for a while. The key

still hung on a hook in the hall. So the reason he was ringing today was to tell Rick's mum that someone else was interested in renting the workshop. The interested man was working away for the next month or so. When he got back, he was going to call in and pick up the key so that he could go and have a look at the place.

Rick found all this out when he got home that lunchtime.

'Your dad's got such a nerve!' his mum grumbled. 'Ringing me up asking me to hand out *his* key. Why should *I* do anything for him?'

Her voice sounded funny. As if she'd caught the twins' cold. She hadn't. Her eyes were red, too, and Rick knew she'd been crying. She missed his dad. She'd never stopped missing him.

'If anyone calls for the key, *I'll* give it to them,' he said. 'Then you won't have to.'

His mum looked at him for a moment, thinking. She sniffed. Then, 'Thanks, Rick,' she said, shaking her head, 'but no. Do you know what? No one's getting their hands on that key. No one.'

With that, she marched through the hall and grabbed the key from the hook. Then she headed for the kitchen and the back door. Rick was right behind her.

'Mum?' he asked. 'Mum, what are you doing?'

'This,' she said.

She drew her arm back and, as hard as she could, she hurled the key towards the bottom of the garden. The lawn nearer the house was neatly mown. Rick's mum had only cut it a week or so before. But down at the bottom, there was just the compost heap and a mass of overgrown grass and weeds. The tangle wasn't as thick as it was in the summer, but it was bad enough.

The key flew into it and disappeared.

'What did you do that for?' Rick cried.

His mum rubbed her hands on the front of her jeans as if she was trying to wipe them clean after they'd touched something dirty. 'Like I said,' she replied, 'why should I do *anything* for your dad?'

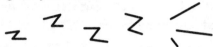

Rick woke up suddenly in the middle of the night. He'd fallen asleep thinking about the dog in Makepiece Avenue. How on earth could he rescue him if his mum wouldn't let him bring the poor thing home? Clyde and Kevin were no help. They couldn't care less. They'd even laughed and said that if he was going to start getting all soppy, then maybe he should join Topz.

When Rick opened his eyes, there was just one thought in his head. His dad had a workshop on an industrial estate just down the road. It would be empty for at least the next month. It was perfect. He could take the dog from the garden, walk him to the workshop, and that's where he'd look after him till he could find somewhere else.

There was only one problem. His mum had thrown away the key.

Wide awake, Rick reached for his alarm clock and pressed the light button. The face glowed. It was three o'clock in the morning. He slipped out of bed and peered through his curtains. The street lamps shone orange along the pavement. It was hard to see past their brightness into the night sky, but he couldn't see the moon or any stars. They must have been hidden behind the same blanket of cloud that had hung in the sky for the last few days.

Rick sat on his bed, thinking. He needed that key. How would he ever find it? The end of their garden was a mess. Even if he hunted for it in broad daylight, the chances were he'd never see it again.

But he *couldn't* hunt for it in broad daylight, could he? Not when his mum would see what he was doing. He'd have to search in the dark. In the middle of the night.

Now.

Tiptoeing to his bedroom door, Rick opened it just a crack and listened. Sometimes Alesha could be restless at night. Especially if she had a cold as she and her sister had now. He could hear the sound of the twins' breathing coming from the bedroom opposite his. They snorted noisily through their stuffed up noses. But they were breathing deeply, too. He was sure they were asleep.

The rest of the house seemed quiet. Still. Rick peered along the landing. He knew his mum sometimes sat up in bed reading if she couldn't sleep, but there was no light coming from her doorway.

Ducking back into his room, he grabbed a fleece from his cupboard and pulled it on. Then, as silently as he could, he crept downstairs.

At the kitchen door, he pressed carefully down on the handle. The door squeaked a little on its hinges as he pushed it open. **Rick froze.** His eyes shot to the stairs. He waited … listened … but there was no movement on the landing.

Once inside the kitchen, Rick pushed the door to behind him. There was no squeak this time. He flicked the light on – gently, so as not to make too much of a click with the switch. Then he started searching the drawers next to the cooker. His mum kept a torch in one of them … There it was in the second drawer down. Would it be working? He pressed the button. Yes! A whitish-yellow beam sprang out. It wasn't very bright but it would have to do.

Turning off the kitchen light, Rick made for the back door. He slipped his bare feet into the trainers he'd left there, turned the key, and stepped out into the garden.

Even though there was no moonlight, it wasn't as dark as Rick had thought it would be. The gleam from the street lamps at the front of the house washed over the roof and the garden seemed to glow slightly. With the torch, too, there was just about enough light to cut through the shadows.

As he reached the weed patch where his mum had thrown the key, Rick glanced over his shoulder back at the house. There were no lights in any of the windows. He hadn't disturbed anyone. That was good. Now it was a matter of searching.

Rick's mum had thrown the key just about in a straight line from the back door. He had seen that much. That meant it should have landed among the weeds right opposite. He decided to concentrate on that patch first.

He crouched down, holding the torch close to the ground. Pulling apart the clumps of grass, leaves and brambles, he shone the light right in amongst them. He tugged and raked with his fingers. Thorns kept scratching at his skin. It hurt. Once he almost cried out, just managing to stop himself. Dirt dug its way under his fingernails. His thumb was bleeding.

But he wouldn't give up.

This was for the dog … *His* dog.

In Rick's mind, the dog wasn't Graham's any more.

Graham wasn't taking care of him. He wasn't giving him the love and attention he needed. He didn't even take him for walks. Graham didn't deserve a dog. No. He was Rick's now.

Suddenly, something lying on the clumpy earth glinted. Right up close to the fence. Rick sucked in a breath and squinted down. Was it? … *Was it?* … Yes, it was! The key! There, picked out in the torchlight! He could hardly believe his eyes. He had never thought it would be that easy to find.

Grabbing it, he stuffed it carefully into the pocket of his fleece and zipped it up. He waved the torch backwards and forwards over the weed patch. It was a bit flattened where he'd pushed his way into it. He shook the tangle of grass and leaves upright again as much as he could. If his mum noticed anything, she'd probably think a neighbour's cat had been in there. They had enough of them prowling through their garden.

Rick headed back to the house. The hand he had used for hunting was covered in mud from the weed patch. He couldn't wash it in case he woke anyone with the sound of running water from the tap. He used his clean hand – the one that held the torch – to push open the back door and return the torch to the drawer.

When he finally clambered into bed, he pulled a glove onto the dirty hand so that he wouldn't leave any smudges on the bedclothes.

Rick was happy. He had the key to his dad's workshop.

And tomorrow? Tomorrow would be a great day – the day he would rescue his dog.

Nine

'Sarah!'

Sarah and Josie turned. They were giving Gruff a morning walk in the park. Benny was yelling at them from the skateboard area.

'I got a postcard from John! He says they found Wales!'

Paul was standing beside him. 'I got a postcard from John, too!' he shouted. 'He says they found Mount Snowdon as well but only because it's *really* big and hard to miss.'

Dave was there with the other two, a skateboard under his arm. He joined in: 'On my postcard, John just says he's hungry all the time!'

None of this was news to Sarah. She'd had regular updates from John on the phone each time he rang to check on Gruff. But he'd sent her a postcard, too. He'd written one for each of the Topz Gang – sisters included.

As the girls headed back out of the park, they saw Dixons in the distance. Only Kevin and Clyde, though. Sarah looked around to see if she could spot Rick. There was no sign of him.

'I think they might have had a fallout,' Josie remarked. 'I keep seeing Kevin and Clyde, but no Rick.'

Sarah wondered where he was. She'd been talking to God about him – asking for another chance to speak to him – but she hadn't seen him since that day outside the corner shop. It was a shame.

She glanced briefly back at Kevin and Clyde. She wasn't sure whether they'd seen her and Josie or not. In any case, they seemed to have lost interest in Gruff.

Then, as the girls were crossing the road, suddenly,

there Rick was, coming out of the newsagents. He was opening a packet of crisps and he looked really fed up.

Sarah's face brightened. 'Rick! Hi!' she called, and waved at him.

He glanced up and scowled.

'Sarah!' Josie nudged her. 'What are you doing?'

'It's all right,' Sarah smiled. 'He was really nice the other day. Let's go and have a chat.'

She started to walk towards him. Rick instantly spun round and began to march the other way.

'Rick!' she called after him again. 'Rick, is everything OK?'

He didn't answer, just strode off even faster.

Josie grabbed Sarah's arm. 'Sarah, stop it,' she said. 'He doesn't look in the mood for chatting. I really think you should leave him alone.'

Sarah watched Rick as he hurried away down the street. She was disappointed. After last time, she thought he'd come over and say hello; give her a friendly wave at least.

But friendly was the last thing Rick looked. It spoilt her morning.

Rick's morning was spoilt, too. Not because of Sarah. Because of Graham. As Rick munched his way through his bag of crisps, he headed moodily back towards Makepiece Avenue. Graham had ruined all his plans for the day.

For some reason that morning, he hadn't gone to work.

Rick had got up early. He should have felt tired after his wakeful night but he didn't. He was excited.

The first thing he did was check that the key to his dad's workshop was still safely in the pocket of his fleece. Next, he pulled a belt from the top drawer of his chest and stuffed it in the other pocket. He didn't have a dog lead so the belt would have to do till he could get hold of one. Then he zipped downstairs before anyone else and grabbed a couple of empty ice cream cartons from a cupboard in the kitchen. His mum kept a pile of them for storing things in. They'd make good food and water bowls. He stuffed them in a carrier bag and put them just outside the front door. He'd take them with him when he left.

Back upstairs, he had a quick shower and scrubbed the dirt from last night's hunt in the weed patch from under his fingernails. Then he threw on his clothes and went out.

'You haven't had breakfast,' his mum called after him.

'Not hungry,' he answered cheerfully.

Ten minutes later, Rick was unlocking the metal sliding door to his dad's workshop. He was sure it would be safe for the dog there, but he wanted to check what sort of state it was in before he went and fetched him. He looked over his shoulder to make sure no one was around, then slipped inside, found the light switch, and slid the door closed behind him.

The workshop stood at the end of a narrow lane just off the main road through the industrial estate. The building next door also happened to be empty and there was a 'To Let' sign outside. The only other building along the lane was used for storage, so there shouldn't be people coming and going all the time. Rick was pleased to think it would be quite easy to keep his dog here. There wouldn't really be anyone around to notice.

Standing in the large, empty space, he looked all around him. It was strange being inside the workshop again. He hadn't been here for months. It must have been well over a year. Probably nearer two. It didn't seem as big as he remembered somehow. But then he was younger and smaller the last time he'd been there with his dad, so it would have looked different. The smell, though, the thick stench of old oil that filled the air – that was exactly the same.

A few half-empty cans of spray paint were clustered on one of the shelves and there was a bucket in one corner. Apart from that, everything had been cleared out. There was nothing left on the workbenches and the concrete floor had been swept. The man who'd been renting the workshop had left it neat and tidy. Even the sink had been thoroughly cleaned. A fat roll of green paper towelling stood on the draining board.

Just about the dirtiest thing in the building was the window that ran along the back wall. It was covered in grime and there were finger marks on the glass at the places where it opened. Rick couldn't help wondering if any of the marks had been made by his dad.

He took the two ice cream cartons he'd brought with him out of the carrier bag. He filled up one with water from the sink, then put them both down on the floor side by side. Seeing them like that made him smile: there would soon be dog food in the empty one. And there would soon be a dog eating from it too, he thought.

Rick glanced at his watch. It was almost eight o'clock. He'd been going to Makepiece Avenue every morning for the last few days. He knew that by nine o'clock,

Graham had always left for work. He also knew that at nine o'clock today, he would be able to rescue his dog.

Stuffing the empty carrier bag into his pocket, he locked the workshop carefully behind him and headed for the corner shop. It was still early, so he didn't think there was any danger of bumping into Dixons. Or Topz for that matter. He bought some cans of dog food and another box of biscuits, which he dropped off at the workshop before heading out again for the avenue.

Once there, he planned to make a big fuss of his dog over the fence. Then he'd wait in the alley for Graham to leave for work.

But this particular morning, that's not what happened. The blue car didn't move from the front of the house. Graham went nowhere.

Rick waited and waited, fondling the dog's ears as the animal nosed at him through the fence. Listening for the sound of a car starting up. 'There's a good boy. It won't be long now,' he smiled.

After an hour or so, Kevin and Clyde stepped into the alley at the other end. They were probably on their way to the park. Rick heard their voices before he saw them. He slipped quickly out and hid round the corner in the avenue. He didn't want them to see him. He didn't want them to ask what he was doing.

Nobody must know. It was his secret.

A while later, when Rick was once again waiting in the alley, he heard Graham come out into the garden through a back door. He was throwing rubbish away. Rick recognised the plastic snap of a wheelie bin's lid closing. The dog disappeared back through the hedge for a moment.

Just before the back door clicked shut again, Rick

heard Graham's voice: 'No, off you go. Not in the house.'

That was all he said. In a moment the dog was back at the fence.

'It's all right boy,' Rick murmured, ruffling his ears once more. 'You don't need to go in that house anyway. I've got somewhere much better for you.'

Another half an hour went by. Still the blue car hadn't moved. Rick kept checking. Every now and then, someone would walk through the alley, and he'd saunter off, sometimes into the avenue, sometimes towards the main road. He couldn't have anyone thinking he was just hanging around.

Time passed slowly. By now, he was getting hungry. He was annoyed, too. Graham usually went to work before nine o'clock. Rick had seen him leave in the dark blue car on the last few mornings. Why hadn't he gone today?

Suddenly it came to him. **Shift work!** The lady he'd met outside Graham's house the other day had told Rick he did *shift work*! That meant the time he went to work changed. He wouldn't always be leaving for his job at the hospital first thing in the morning.

How could Rick have forgotten that? He was angry with himself. He kicked out at the alley wall. Supposing Graham wasn't going in till much later today? Worse, what if he had the day off and wasn't going in at all?

Rick wanted to get the dog away from him. He was ready to go now. How much longer would he have to wait? **? ? ?**

By eleven o'clock, Rick was starving. He had a bit of change left from buying the dog food, so he decided to go to the newsagents for a bag of crisps. It wouldn't take him long and by the time he got back, Graham would be gone, wouldn't he? Even if he hadn't gone to work, couldn't he just be gone?

As Rick stepped back out of the newsagents opening the bag of crisps, he heard someone calling him. *Great.* It was Sarah from the Topz Gang. What did she think she was doing, shouting to him as if they were best mates? He'd asked her a few questions about looking after dogs, that's all. It didn't mean he wanted to talk to her now. It didn't mean he'd *ever* want to talk to her.

Sarah was starting to walk towards him. Her friend, Josie, was with her. Rick twisted round and strode off in the other direction. If she tried to follow him, he'd tell her to get lost.

She didn't. When he glanced over his shoulder, she and Josie had gone.

Good ...

Back in Makepiece Avenue, Rick caught his breath. There was an empty space in the road outside Number One. He felt his heart beat faster. At last, Graham's blue car had gone.

Rick dodged into the alley, crouched close up to the fence and called softly. 'Hey! It's me! Here boy, come here!' For a moment nothing happened. There was no sound or movement. Then the dog's dark shape appeared behind the hedge and the next moment, his black nose was pushing through it.

Rick glanced up and down the alley. There was no one around, but he'd have to be quick.

He unzipped his fleece pocket and took out the belt

he'd put there. Looping it through the dog's red collar, he carefully did up the buckle, wrapped the other end around his hand and held it firmly in his fist. Then he grabbed the top of the wire fence and pulled it down as far as he could. It wasn't difficult. The hedge was pushing it over anyway.

The dog shoved himself forwards.

In a moment, he was free.

Rick gasped in excitement. The dog jumped up at him wagging his tail. Rick found himself laughing out loud. He couldn't help it.

That's when he heard the footsteps. They were walking along the pavement that led into the avenue. Getting closer to the entrance to the alley. Closer to where he stood with the dog!

Rick held his breath. He hunched down, pulling the animal to him. 'Sssh!' he hissed softly, willing the dog to be quiet and still.

The person strolled by. It was a man with his hands stuffed in his pockets. He had a newspaper under one arm and headphones tucked into his ears. He didn't stop; didn't look down the alley. In a second, he'd ambled past.

Rick still didn't move. He huddled there with the dog, listening. The footsteps died away. The man had gone.

With one last glance over his shoulder, Rick stood up. The dog was already eagerly straining at his makeshift lead. Rick watched him for a moment. Then, *My dog*, he thought happily, and the two of them stepped out of the alley.

Ten

Next morning, Sarah was still having breakfast when the phone rang. Her dad was about to leave for work, but he stopped to answer it on his way out. Sarah was sure it would be John.

'Can you tell him I'm taking Gruff out in a minute?' she mumbled through a mouth full of cereal. 'I'm waiting for Josie. And could you maybe ask him to *stop* ringing so early? He always phones when I'm trying to eat my breakfast.'

Her dad shook his head and held the receiver out. 'It's not John,' he said.

'Hi, Sarah, it's Josie.' Her friend's voice spoke cheerfully down the phone. 'I suddenly remembered I've got a violin lesson this morning. Really sorry, but I won't be able to come with you and Gruff. Will you be all right by yourself?'

Sarah didn't mind going out on her own. In fact, if she bumped into Rick, it might be a good thing that Josie wasn't there. Perhaps that's why he'd walked away from her yesterday. Maybe he didn't want to talk to her with Josie there, too.

Outside, it was warm. Perhaps the first really warm spring morning since the start of the school holidays. The sun shone yellow in a clear sky.

Sarah decided to walk Gruff towards the shopping centre. She'd been going to the park every day. A change of direction would be good.

As they got nearer, she spotted the sign for the industrial estate pointing off to the left. It reminded her of the stretch of grass John had mentioned near the supermarket. She hadn't been that way for ages. She could give Gruff a run there.

Turning at the sign, Sarah began to walk along the wide pavement. She passed several large buildings. They were oblong-shaped, with flat roofs, enormous doors and lines of windows high up in the walls. There was the noise of machinery, and some kind of smell, a bit like paint, that caught in Sarah's throat. She wrinkled her nose, walking more quickly to try and leave it behind.

Up ahead, she could see someone else striding along. A tall boy wearing a red fleece. He looked a lot like Rick, Sarah thought. But the boy in front of her was walking a dog. Rick didn't have a dog so it couldn't be him.

Suddenly, the boy turned off the main road. As Sarah got closer, she could see the entrance to a narrow lane. She glanced down it as she and Gruff walked by. At the far end, the boy was unlocking the door to a workshop. He slid it back and disappeared inside with the dog.

Sarah stopped still.

The boy *was* Rick. She was sure of it. But Rick had said his mum didn't want him to have a dog. How could he be out walking with one? Sarah's mind whizzed through the possibilities: perhaps his mum had changed her mind. Perhaps he was walking a dog for someone else. Whatever the reason, Sarah was pleased for him. When she'd last talked to him, he'd seemed to want one so badly.

Sarah hesitated. What she really wanted to do now was go and say hello. That would be all right, wouldn't it? She could ask Rick about the dog. He must be really excited. She could even suggest showing him the grass near the supermarket. They could take the dogs there together.

She'd been praying for another chance to talk to him. Perhaps this was it.

Gruff gave a tug on his lead. He wanted to get going. Sarah still didn't move.

A moment later, Rick reappeared out of the workshop. He didn't have the dog with him this time. Sarah heard him say something, then slide the door shut and lock it. Rick didn't spot her until he turned.

For one moment, he looked surprised. Then his eyes seemed to darken with anger. Furiously, he marched towards her.

Sarah backed away slightly. He didn't look at all how he had when they'd chatted outside the shop. He looked the way he usually did.

Like a Dixon.

'Are you following me?' he growled when he got up close.

Sarah shook her head. 'Following you? No, of course I'm not!'

'I don't believe you!' he snapped. 'What are you doing here then?'

'I was just taking Gruff for a walk, that's all,' Sarah gulped. 'There's some grass up here. I thought he could have a run.'

'He could have a run in the park,' Rick hissed.

'I – I know,' Sarah stammered. 'I just thought I'd take him somewhere different.'

Rick pushed his face close to hers. 'Well, you can take him away again, can't you?'

Sarah nodded. Then, 'It's just that I saw you with a dog and I didn't know if you might want to walk them together,' she blurted out.

It was Rick's turn to step back. 'You didn't see me

with a dog.'

Sarah looked at him, not understanding. 'Yes, I did,' she said quietly. 'A black one. I was happy for you. I thought maybe your mum had said you could have one after all.'

She could see Rick was thinking hard. He was pulling at his top lip with his fingers; chewing at it with his teeth.

'Yeah, well, it's not my dog,' he said at last. 'I'm just … looking after him for someone.'

'Well, that's good,' Sarah replied. 'At least you get to spend time with a dog. Even if it's not yours.' She paused. 'You could still walk him with Gruff and me if you wanted to,' she added timidly.

Rick shook his head. 'I can't.'

There was silence. Sarah waited for Rick to say something else. He didn't.

'Right,' she mumbled.

Turning, she started to walk off. Not towards the grass. She went the other way. Back towards the shopping centre and away from the industrial estate. She was shaking. Rick was scary when he was angry.

That wasn't the worst of it, though. The worst thing was that whatever chance she'd had to make friends with a Dixons boy at long last had vanished clean away. Sarah stung inside.

'Hang on!'

She heard Rick call but was half afraid to turn around in case it wasn't to her. She didn't want him to shout at her again.

'Sarah, wait!'

Slowly, she looked back.

'If you want to say hello to the dog, you can,' Rick muttered. 'You may as well. You've seen him anyway.'

Sarah hesitated. 'I don't have to.'

'I said you can, though, didn't I?' Rick grunted.

At the end of the lane, Rick fished the key to the workshop out of his pocket and unlocked the door again. The black dog inside ran towards him. He sprang up on his hind legs and rested his paws near the boy's shoulders.

Gruff pulled forward on his lead excitedly. When the other dog saw him, he dropped down, and the two of them sniffed curiously at each other. Gruff was much smaller but far more confident. The bigger dog kept backing off, then creeping forward again nervously. Sarah noticed how his red collar stood out against his black hair. When she spotted his one white foot, she couldn't help smiling.

'Oh, he's gorgeous!' she exclaimed. 'What's his name?'

Rick threw her a glance. What *was* his name? Rick didn't know. He'd never heard Graham use it. All Rick had been calling him was 'dog' or 'boy'. He didn't actually have a name for him.

He said the first thing he could think of. The best name for a dog: 'Wolf, **he's called Wolf.'**

'That's a cool name,' Sarah grinned. 'So, what do you have to do? Just take him for walks? Is this his owner's workshop?'

Once again, Rick didn't know how to answer. For a moment, he said nothing. Then, slowly he shook his head.

'This is my dad's workshop,' he said.

'Your dad's?'

Rick nodded. 'The thing is, I *am* looking after Wolf, but I'm doing it because he needs someone. Not for anyone else.'

'What do you mean?' Sarah asked. 'Who's is he?'

'He's mine,' Rick said finally. 'There's this man and he doesn't want him any more. He hasn't got time for him. So he's given him to me.'

Sarah frowned. 'But, I thought your mum didn't want you to have a dog?'

'She doesn't. She doesn't know anything about him. That's why I've brought him here.' He watched Sarah's eyes widen. 'Well, what's wrong with that?' he demanded. 'Dad's gone and no one else is using the place at the moment. The dog – Wolf – wasn't being taken care of. So now I'm going to look after him here.'

'Does the man who gave him to you know you're not allowed to keep him at home?'

'It's got nothing to do with him,' Rick shrugged. 'He wouldn't care anyway. He doesn't want him and I do.'

Sarah watched the black dog. He and Gruff were still nosing at each other.

'How long has he been here?' Sarah said, remembering all the questions Rick had asked her about dogs. Perhaps he'd had Wolf then. Perhaps he'd been keeping him at the workshop for a few days.

'Only since yesterday,' Rick replied. 'It was his first night here last night. He was all right, though. And I came out really early and took him for a walk.'

Sarah looked all round at the dingy space. She saw the two ice cream tubs on the concrete floor. One was empty, the other full of water. But there was nothing else that was good for a dog. No bed for him to lie on.

'Wolf can't stay here for long, Rick,' she said gently. 'It's just not right for him.'

Suddenly, the Dixons boy looked desperate. 'It's fine, all right?' he said. 'I'll take him out loads. I'll stay here with him as much as I can.'

'Yes, but in a few days the holidays are over. You'll be back at school.'

'I won't go to school, then,' Rick snapped. 'It's not like I haven't bunked off before. I'd sooner be with Wolf anyway.'

Sarah put out her hand to stroke Wolf's head. 'You're going to have to tell your mum,' she said softly.

'No.'

'Then I'll talk to *my* mum and dad. They'll know what's the best thing to do.'

'No!' Rick shouted it this time. 'You don't tell anyone, do you hear me? No one can know, Sarah! *Not ever!*'

Eleven

Sarah almost ran with Gruff all the way home.

When she burst in through the front door, her mum looked at her hot, red cheeks and ruffled hair.

'Everything all right?' she asked.

Sarah nodded. She unclipped Gruff's lead, too breathless to speak.

'Well, when you've got your breath back,' her mum said, 'can you ring John on Uncle Tom's mobile? He just wants a word.'

'Oh, what does he want *now*?' she puffed. 'Well, it'll have to be later. There's something I've got to do.'

'He'll only ring again if you don't get back to him,' her mum replied. 'You know what he's like.'

'OK, I will in a bit.'

Her mum frowned. 'Are you sure you're all right?'

'I'm *fine*,' Sarah insisted.

She dashed upstairs to her bedroom, pushed the door closed and flopped down on her bed. Saucy, her cat, was lying on her pillow. Sarah gave her a quick scratch behind the ears and sat still for a moment trying to calm down.

Then she closed her eyes.

Actually, I'm not fine at all, God. Please help me. I've got a secret and I don't know what to do. I can't tell anyone. Not Mum or Dad or John. Not even Josie. Only You.

Rick's hiding a dog. Wolf. He's trying to be kind by looking after him. You can see how much he cares about him, God. I think he really loves him. But he's keeping Wolf in a dirty old workshop where it's cold and dark. Rick can't stay with him all the time through the day, and Wolf has to be on his own at night. Rick says that when term starts, he'll bunk off school to keep him company, but he can't. He'll get in so much trouble.

And he doesn't have any money either, God. How's he going to be able to buy Wolf's food? How will he be able to go to the vet if Wolf gets ill?

I told him he should tell his mum, but he won't. He says if she knows, she'll make him give Wolf back to his owner. But he says he can't give him back. He says Wolf was just left out in the garden. Out in the rain. 'How can you give an animal back to someone who doesn't care about it?' he said. 'You can't.'

Then he looked really sad. 'I know how it feels not to be cared about,' he said. 'To be left on your own. It feels bad. Really, really horrible. And I'm not going to let that happen to Wolf.'

He's talking about him and his dad, God, I know he is. I wish I could help him understand that even though his dad's gone away, You're always here. You want to love him and be part of his life. You want to help him stop hurting.

It's funny, but it's almost as if Rick's trying to stop hurting by looking after Wolf – looking after something

*else that needs love and attention like he does.
But You're the only one who can really help, aren't You,
God?*

*God, please help Rick to find You. Please help him see
that he doesn't have to be on his own. Your love never
changes. It never stops. His dad may have gone away,
but You'll **never** go.*

*I've said I'll help him with Wolf. I'm really scared and I
don't know if it's the right thing to do, but that's what
I've said so I'll do it. I've **got** to. And I'm telling You,
God, because You're the only One I **can** tell. You're the
only One who can help me.*

I need You, God. I need You so much ...

Sarah's eyes opened. Her gaze fell on Saucy who was
fast asleep beside her. 'Look at you,' she murmured,
reaching out a finger to stroke the soft fur above
the little cat's nose. 'I can't bear it when I think that
someone abandoned you. Just left you all on your own.'

When Saucy was a kitten, she'd been dumped behind
a rubbish bin in a cardboard box. Sarah and her family
had brought her home from the rescue centre. It was a
long time ago, but there were still
days when Sarah would look at
Saucy and find her eyes filling with
tears. How could someone have
done that? She was so fluffy and
floppy, and needing to be loved.

*That's what everyone wants,
isn't it?* Sarah thought. *Love.*

That's why I've got to help Rick and Wolf.

Sarah twisted round on the bed and reached for her moneybox. It was shaped like a cat and painted red with swirls of gold and green. She opened it up, pulled out two five pound notes, then shook it. Three one pound coins fell onto the bed and there were some ten pence pieces as well. She gathered all the money up and stuffed it into her purse.

As she did so, she could hear the phone start to ring.

'Sarah!' her mum called up the stairs. 'It's for you. Guess who?'

The last person Sarah felt like talking to was John. As usual, he'd want to know how Gruff was getting on. Was he eating all his food? Was he enjoying his walks? She could deal with that. She didn't mind that he kept asking. It was annoying but it didn't matter.

But there was another question that he almost always asked; that she just didn't know how to answer today: *Have you seen Dixons?*

'Gruff's fine,' Sarah said into the phone. 'I mean, I'm sure he misses you and everything, John, but he's eating really well and he's happy when we go out, so you honestly don't need to keep ringing. If there was a problem, I'd tell you,' she added quickly, hoping that would stop him from asking anything else.

It didn't.

'What about Dixons? Are they keeping out of your way?'

Sarah sighed. 'I'm not worried about Dixons,' she said. 'Nor is Gruff.'

'And Rick? Has he spoken to you again?'

Sarah closed her eyes. She'd told John how Rick had talked to her outside the shop. She'd been so excited.

Now, she wished she'd never mentioned it.

'No,' she replied quietly.

'That's good,' John said cheerfully. 'I know you said he seemed nice the other day, but I still think you should be careful.'

'I *will* be.'

When Sarah put the phone down, she felt miserable. What was happening to her? First, she was keeping a secret she probably shouldn't keep.

Now she'd told a lie.

She'd hardly finished talking to John when the phone rang again.

'Hi, Sarah, it's Josie. Sorry I couldn't do a walk this morning. Actually, it probably would have been better if I'd missed my violin lesson. I was rubbish today. Couldn't play a thing in tune. Were you OK? No Dixons trouble?'

'I was fine,' Sarah answered flatly. She was getting tired of saying it.

'Anyway, I just wondered if you wanted to come over. Mum says you can bring Gruff. Then we can take him for a walk from here later.'

'I can't, Josie, I'm sorry,' Sarah said. 'I'm a bit busy now.'

'OK,' Josie replied. 'Well, let me know when you're going for a walk and I'll come round.'

'Thanks.'

There was a pause. Then, 'Are you all right?' Josie asked.

'Of course I'm all right,' Sarah muttered, trying not to sound irritated. 'Everyone keeps asking me if I'm all right. I *am* all right. Honestly.'

'OK then,' said Josie. 'See you later, Sarah.'

Sarah glanced at the clock in the hall. In about an hour's time, she'd arranged to meet Rick back at the workshop.

She had told him she'd get some more food for Wolf. She'd buy him a proper water bowl, too. He could easily knock over the ice cream cartons and she didn't like to think that he'd be in the workshop all night without any water.

She ran upstairs, grabbed her purse and dropped it into her bag.

'Mum!' she called. 'I'm just going to take Gruff to the shopping centre. Is there anything you want me to get?'

'You're taking him out *again*?' her mum asked. 'You haven't been back long.'

'I know,' she nodded, 'but I'm not doing anything else, so I may as well.'

Sarah was glad her mum didn't want any shopping. She wasn't sure she'd be able to carry much more than she already planned to buy.

Her first stop was one of the charity shops. She left Gruff tied up outside while she went in to hunt out some bedding for Wolf. She bought four large cushions and two blankets. She and Rick could spread them on the floor in the workshop, then Wolf wouldn't have to lie on the concrete any more.

Next, awkwardly lugging the big plastic sack full of bedding, she went into the pet shop and found a water bowl. That took most of the rest of her money. There wasn't enough left now for dog food. Never mind. Rick said he'd got plenty for a day or two. She could worry about that another time.

Soon, Sarah was standing with Gruff outside the workshop again. She looked back up the lane. There was no one to see her.

'Rick!' she called softly. 'Rick, it's me. Sarah.'

A moment later, the door opened.

Twelve

Rick was quiet.

'What's wrong?' Sarah asked. 'Has something happened? Does your mum know?'

He shook his head. 'It's you, isn't it?' he mumbled. He glanced at the bed Sarah had made up for Wolf on the floor. **'I can't believe you bought all this stuff for Wolf.'**

'It's only so he'll be comfortable,' she said. 'It can't be very nice lying on concrete.'

'I'll pay you back.'

'You don't have to, you know.'

'I will, though,' Rick insisted. 'As soon as I've got some money, I'll give it back to you.'

There was a pause. Then, 'My dad took our dog,' he muttered. 'When he left. I didn't tell you that, did I?'

Sarah frowned. She hadn't even thought of that as a possibility. When Rick told her they used to have a dog, she assumed the poor thing must have died.

'No,' she murmured. 'Rick, I'm so sorry. Do you ever get to see him? You must really miss him … *and* your dad.'

Rick's eyes flicked towards her. 'Why would I waste my time missing my dad? He doesn't miss *me*, does he?'

'I'm sure he does.'

'What do you mean?' Rick was glaring at her. 'Why would you say that? Do you know my dad?'

'No, but – '

'Then you can't say that, can you?' he snapped.

Sarah fell silent.

'You Topz are all the same,' Rick began again. 'It's all right for *you*, isn't it? You've all got everything you want.

Your lovey-dovey families, your friends, your pets. You think you're so perfect, saying your prayers like good little kiddies. It's all so easy for you, isn't it?' He scowled as he spoke. 'Well, *my* life's not easy. Do you have any idea what it's like to have your dad just get up and go? To have your mum cross all the time?'

Sarah shook her head. 'No,' she said softly. 'But I can try and understand ... If you want me to.'

'Yeah, right,' Rick scoffed.

'Anyway ...,' Sarah added. She had to say something now. If she didn't, she knew she never would. 'Anyway, whatever kind of family you're from, whatever your life's like ...'

'What?'

'God cares about you.'

At that, Rick turned away. He didn't want to hear it, but Sarah hadn't finished.

'There's a verse in the Bible that says, "... *even the hairs of your head have all been counted.*" Do you know what that means, Rick?' Sarah went on insistently. 'It means that God knows absolutely everything about you. He knows how many hairs there are growing on your head! Who else knows that? I bet you can't name anyone. I bet you don't even know yourself! But the amazing thing is every single one of those hairs is important to God! He loves you and He cares about what happens to you.' She paused. 'He cares about what happens to Wolf, too. He wants to help.'

The Dixons boy swung back. His teeth were clamped together, his fists clenched. As he turned on Sarah, his eye fell on the heap of cushions and blankets she had bought for Wolf. He wanted to be angry with her; to tell her to shut up, to go away, anything.

But, he couldn't. Sarah had been kind to Wolf. She might be winding him up; talking when she should just keep quiet. But he was grateful. So he didn't say anything.

'You haven't ever seen my cat, have you, Rick?' Sarah said. 'God cares about her, too, I know He does. We got her from the rescue centre when she was just a little kitten. Can you believe what someone had done? They'd dumped her in a cardboard box and left her behind a rubbish bin. But she was found and now she's living with us. I'm sure that God was looking out for her. He wants to look out for me and you, too. You've just got to let Him ...'

There was silence. Sarah waited – half hopeful, half nervous – but the Dixons boy continued to say nothing. He just stared at the floor grimly.

'We could take Wolf and Gruff for a walk now if you like,' Sarah suggested after a long pause. 'Be good for them to go out together.'

'I'm not going to the park,' Rick answered bluntly. 'I can't, can I? Someone'll see me. Mum can't find out.'

'I didn't mean to the park. I mean around here. There's that grass I told you about a bit further up the road. I don't think anyone goes there much. I could show you.'

Rick eyed her suspiciously. Then he glanced back at Wolf. The black dog had been sniffing at his new bed cautiously. He must have decided it was safe because he'd finally flopped down on top of it. His nose rested between his front paws.

Rick nodded slowly. 'OK,' he agreed. 'I reckon he'd like a walk on a bit of grass.'

They stepped out of the workshop with the dogs and

Rick locked the door behind them. Sarah glanced at the belt he'd attached to Wolf's collar.

'We need to get him a proper lead,' she said.

'I'll get one soon,' was all Rick replied.

They walked to the end of the lane, then turned left and went on up the road in silence. Sarah decided to keep quiet. If she asked any questions, Rick clammed up anyway. Either that or the things she said made him angry. She didn't like it when he turned on her.

Wolf and Gruff seemed happy enough to be together. They looked quite funny trotting along side by side, Sarah thought. Wolf with his long, sleek legs; Gruff with his short, stubby ones.

Up ahead lay the stretch of grass near the supermarket where Gruff sometimes went with John. Just as Sarah had said, there was no one about. Cars and vans trundled past now and again, but she and Rick had passed most of the buildings so this end of the industrial estate was always quite peaceful.

Gruff began to pull on his lead. Wolf did the same. He seemed to sense there was something more interesting than tarmac streets in front of them. The four of them crossed the road and, once on the grass, the two dogs thrust their noses down, sniffing enthusiastically.

'Maybe we shouldn't let them off the leads,' Sarah said. 'It's a bit close to the road and we don't know whether Wolf will come back when you call him.'

She waited for Rick to respond, but he said nothing. As they walked, her gaze slid from the Dixons boy to the blank, white, windowless wall that formed the back of the supermarket. It looked harsh and ugly against the soft green of the grass. It was a shame the shop had been built. It must have looked much prettier when the ground beneath it was still grass. One day, there would probably be buildings on this stretch of green, too. That's what Sarah's dad said.

Gruff stopped to have a good nose at a muddy patch by her feet. Sarah stopped with him.

And suddenly, there he was: a boy with thick, ginger hair, climbing over the wooden fence that separated the supermarket from the grass. Sarah saw him straight away. He was a little way off, but there was no mistaking who it was.

She caught her breath. Rick turned to look at her. Instantly, his eyes followed hers.

'What's *he* doing here?' Rick hissed when he saw Clyde swinging his legs over the fencing and jumping down onto the grass. 'You said no one comes here.'

'I didn't think anyone did,' Sarah gulped. 'Not usually, anyway. Come on, let's just go back. He probably won't see you.'

'Of course he's going to see me!'

'Well, maybe he won't know it's you.'

'He's not stupid, Sarah!' snapped Rick.

Sarah looked down desperately at the two dogs. Then she did the only thing she could think of. She grabbed the belt holding Wolf from Rick, twisted round and started walking briskly away.

'What are you doing?' muttered Rick.

'I'll meet you back at the workshop,' she said, head down as she hurried off.

Sarah didn't have any idea what Rick would say to Clyde. She wasn't worried, though. He'd be able to make something up. Some excuse or other for being on the industrial estate talking to a Topz. That's what he was good at. Excuses. Stories.

The important thing was that he didn't have Wolf with him. Wolf would have been harder to explain away.

She turned down the lane to the workshop to wait for Rick. He could be ages trying to get away from Clyde. However long it took, she'd just have to stay there.

But when he got back, then what? This whole thing was a disaster. If Rick couldn't even take Wolf for a proper walk in case he was seen, how was it ever going to work? Wolf might have been given to him to have a better life. Rick might have believed that's what he could offer him. But he hadn't thought it through. None of it. Wolf seemed to have been taken out of one bad situation and thrown right into another.

Only, this one was worse, Sarah thought. Rick didn't even have enough money to keep buying dog food.

When he finally got back, it was Sarah who was the quiet one. She had no idea what to say.

'I didn't think I'd ever get rid of him,' Rick told her. 'Can you believe it, Clyde said his dad's just got a job at that supermarket! What are the chances of *that*? So I won't be able to take Wolf over that way in case I bump into him again. I told him I'd followed you,' he added. 'I said I wanted to know why you were out walking two dogs. He believed me, too.'

Rick grinned at his own inventiveness.

Sarah didn't grin back. 'I'd better go,' she said. 'Mum'll be wondering where I am.'

She handed him the belt holding Wolf. She turned, pulling Gruff with her, and started to walk away.

'Thanks for what you did back there,' Rick called after her. 'For a minute, I thought I was in trouble.'

Sarah stopped. Glancing back over her shoulder, she said flatly, 'You *are* in trouble, Rick. So is Wolf. You can't look after a dog like this. It's not right. You're going to have to think of something else.'

As she and Gruff carried on down the lane, Rick shouted after her, 'Don't you tell anyone! If you ever tell anyone, I'll never forgive you!'

Sarah kept walking, but there were tears stinging in her eyes.

Thirteen

The next morning the doorbell rang just as Sarah was slipping on her trainers. She looked up. She could see the shape well enough through the frosted glass of the front door to know who it was. Josie.

No! she thought. Sarah had got up extra early to make sure she was out of the house with Gruff before Josie came round. She needed to get over to the workshop. Trying to look after Wolf like this was hopeless, she knew that. At the same time, how could she stop helping?

The doorbell rang again.

'Are you going to answer that, Sarah?' her mum called.

'Yes,' she sighed.

'Hello!' said Josie brightly as she opened the door.

'You're early,' Sarah replied.

'I know, sorry. It's just I'm going out with Mum a bit later, so I thought if I came over now, I'd still get to walk Gruff with you.'

As usual, Gruff had been dashing in circles since he'd seen Sarah reach for her trainers. The circles grew even more excitable when he saw Josie on the doorstep.

'I think Gruff's ready to go even if you're not,' Josie added with a grin.

'No, I'm ready,' said Sarah. 'I was going to take him on my own, that's all. I mean, if you're busy today, you don't have to come with us. We'll be OK. We look after each other, don't we, Gruff?'

'Oh, no,' Josie answered, 'I *want* to come. I rang yesterday afternoon to go with you then, but your mum said you were already out. Didn't she tell you?'

Sarah nodded. 'Yeah, she did.'

'You didn't ring back, though,' said Josie.

'No. Sorry, I had stuff to do.'

Sarah sounded fed up, Josie thought. Cross, almost. She'd been a bit weird on the phone yesterday morning, too.

'Are you sure everything's all right?' Josie asked.

'Why wouldn't it be?' was the answer.

Josie watched as Sarah caught hold of Gruff's collar and clipped on his lead. She and Sarah told each other everything. Why wasn't Sarah talking to her now?

They walked to the park together almost in silence. Josie kept trying to chat, but her friend hardly responded. Sarah was striding out fast along the pavement, too.

'Are we in a hurry?' Josie said, breathlessly.

'No,' Sarah replied.

But Sarah *was* in a hurry. The quicker she could get the walk with Josie done, the quicker she could get over to the industrial estate.

The girls crossed the road and were about to go through the park gates, when Josie stopped. Sarah didn't notice and carried on walking.

'Aww,' she heard Josie say, 'that's such a shame. I hate it when that happens.'

Sarah glanced behind her. Josie was looking at a small, laminated poster that had been tied to a lamp-post.

'What is it?' Sarah asked. She didn't really care. She just wanted to get on.

'Someone's lost their dog. Look.'

Sarah turned round and led Gruff back to Josie.

The first thing she saw was the word 'MISSING' typed in big, red letters across the top of the poster.

The next was the photograph of the lost dog. It was beautiful, with short, black hair and deep brown eyes. Its bright red collar stood out against the darkness of its coat.

'What a lovely dog,' said Josie. 'I wonder what's happened to him.'

Sarah didn't answer. She couldn't stop staring. Couldn't drag her eyes away from the photo. She felt a shiver begin to creep its way along her spine. Like finger tips running up her back.

The poster said the dog's name was Jack.

'He looks like a Jack, doesn't he?' Josie added.

No, thought Sarah. *He doesn't look like a Jack at all. That dog looks exactly like a Wolf.*

Gruff never got his walk in the park.

After seeing the poster, Sarah had hurried straight home with Josie at her heels.

'Sarah, what's wrong? You look awful,' Josie had frowned. Sarah's face was white; her eyes wide and almost frightened.

She'd told Josie she felt sick. She'd have to go.

It wasn't a lie. Sarah *did* feel sick. She felt scared, too. **The missing dog was Wolf,** she was sure of it. Same sleek, black face and shining eyes. Same red collar. The poster said his name was Jack, but that was the only difference.

All the other details fitted perfectly. They said the dog had disappeared the day before yesterday. The day Sarah knew Rick had taken him to the workshop.

The sick feeling churned in her stomach.
How hadn't she guessed it? How stupid was she?
She should have known.

Wolf was stolen! Sarah was helping a Dixons boy look

after a *stolen* dog.

Up in her bedroom, she huddled on her bed, knees hugged up to her chest. Hot tears streaked her cheeks.

She'd left Josie at the front door.

'I'll be all right in a minute,' she'd mumbled.

Her mum had called through from the kitchen, 'Back already?'

Sarah had shot upstairs. She couldn't let her mum see her; couldn't let her know how upset she was. She couldn't let anyone know.

Rocking herself backwards and forwards, Sarah squeezed her eyes closed. She had to try and think straight; try to remember exactly what Rick had told her about Wolf ...

'There's this man and he doesn't want him any more. He hasn't got time for him. So he's given him to me.'

That was what Rick had said. Sarah had believed him.

She sat there in silence. Then the sound of the hoover drifted up the stairs. She tried to block it out. She needed to pray.

What have I done, God? I only wanted to do something good. Dixons hate Topz. They always have. But I thought if I helped Rick, then maybe I could talk to him about You. I thought he might see what a difference You make to me. If he had You as his Friend, it would change his life too, I know it would. He'd feel loved again.

I hoped that if I was kind to him and to Wolf that, well, he might even see You in me.

But he doesn't see anything, does he, God? Just a stupid

girl he can tell lies to and get on his side because she'll believe him so easily.

And now I've helped him do something terrible. I've helped him steal a dog. Well, not steal him maybe, but I've helped Rick hide him.

No wonder he didn't want anyone to know about Wolf. No wonder he's being so secretive. I should have known. I'm such an idiot! But, God, I thought he was trying to save Wolf from someone who didn't care about him. I thought he was doing something kind. Wolf isn't even the dog's name, is it, it's Jack.

And now's Jack's owner's out there – all upset and lonely and miserable. I'm sure he is. He must be worrying about what's happened to his beautiful dog. Wondering if he's all right or not.

And I know where his dog is, don't I, God?

*So what am I going to do? Rick says if I tell anyone he'll never forgive me. But how can I **not** tell anyone now that I know he's been lying to me? Wolf **isn't** his dog. He **has** to give him back. He'll hate me forever if I tell on him, I know he will. I don't expect I'll ever be able to talk to him about You again. I'll probably be in trouble with everyone, too.*

But I know someone out there has lost their beautiful dog. Rick's taken him and he can't even look after him properly. I've got to say something to someone, haven't I, God? I've just got to …

Sarah ran downstairs. Her mum was putting the hoover away.

'Right,' her mum said as she ducked back out of the cupboard. 'What shall I get for lunch?'

Sarah hesitated. 'Actually … is it all right if I just go out again? I won't be long.'

Her mum looked at her carefully. 'Where are you off to this time?'

'Erm …' What could Sarah say? She didn't want to lie, but she couldn't tell the whole truth either. Not yet. 'The thing is,' she went on, 'when I was out with Josie this morning, we saw a poster about a lost dog. I can't stop thinking about it. It looks so lovely in the photo. Do you remember that time when we lost Gruff? It was so horrible, so I know how awful the owner must be feeling. Well, the owner's name and stuff is on the poster. I want to write down the phone number. Then if I hear anything about the dog, I can ring up. I can keep my eyes open for him when I'm out, too.'

Sarah's mum smiled. 'My Sarah,' she said kindly. 'Always trying to make things better for everyone, aren't you?'

Sarah raced to the park. She knew she'd have to be quick if she wasn't going to be back late for lunch. At the lamp-post with the poster on it, she stopped and took out the pen and the scrap of paper she'd stuffed into her pocket. She scribbled down the name, address and phone number of the dog's owner. He lived in Makepiece Avenue. Fortunately, Sarah knew where that was. If she hurried, she'd get there quite quickly.

At the end of the avenue, she stopped. Partly to catch her breath. Partly to look at the 'MISSING' poster on the lamp-post. She'd passed one further down the road, too.

They were the same as down by the park.

She took another few steps until she was standing on the pavement in front of Number One. She saw that the garden gate had come off its hinges and was lying on the ground. The house looked a bit scruffy, too. There was a dark blue car parked in the road outside. Sarah wondered if it belonged to the dog's owner. Then she noticed that one of the 'MISSING' posters had been stuck in its back window.

This must definitely be the house.

She stood still, staring at it. Now she was there, suddenly she didn't know why. What had she come for? What would she say? Would there even be anyone in? She couldn't help hoping there wouldn't be.

Sarah gazed ahead of her blankly for a second more. Then she caught her breath.

The front door opened and a man stepped out.

Fourteen

Josie was worried. Something was definitely wrong. Sarah was acting very strangely.

Josie had seen her in a bad mood before. She knew exactly what Sarah was like when she was miserable. But this was different. And as for what had happened when they were out with Gruff that morning, that was just plain weird.

'I'm telling you, Sarah went white as a sheet,' she said to some of the Topz boys. She'd found them riding their bikes in the park.

'When you say, "white as a sheet",' Paul said, 'how white is that exactly? I mean, not all sheets are white, are they?'

Benny laughed, but Josie was totally serious.

'It's not funny,' she answered. 'I mean it. Something's going on and I don't know what it is.'

'Have you asked her?' Danny said.

'Of course I have,' Josie sighed. 'I've asked if everything's all right, and she says it is. Then this morning, she just said she had to go because she was feeling sick.'

'Well, that's probably it then,' said Benny. 'She's not feeling well. She's got a bug or something.'

'No, you're wrong, Benny. She hasn't got a bug,' Josie insisted. 'She was really looking forward to doing lots of Gruff walks with me while John's away. But now it's as if she doesn't want me there at all.'

'I could call round later, I suppose,' Dave offered. 'I could ask how John's getting on. See if I can find out if anything's happened.'

'Thanks, Dave,' Josie replied. 'But if she won't tell me, I don't see why she'd tell you.'

'Still, it's worth a try.'

Paul nodded. 'Better than doing nothing, isn't it?' he agreed. 'But I don't think you should worry, Josie. Sarah doesn't usually keep quiet if something's bothering her does she?'

'No,' grinned Benny. 'John says she could talk the legs off a fish.'

Josie made a face. 'Benny, fish don't *have* legs,' she said.

'They did until Sarah started talking,' Benny replied. He laughed loudly and jumped back on his bike.

But when Dave called round at Sarah's later that afternoon, she wasn't at home.

'Honestly, Dave,' her mum said, 'I think Gruff's legs are going to be even shorter by the time John gets back. That little dog's never *had* so many walks.'

Dave wondered where Sarah had gone. He'd just come from the park and she wasn't there. She must have gone the other way, to the shopping centre. He thought about cycling over to see, but then decided not to. He could call back at her house later.

Sarah hadn't meant to go to the shopping centre. She'd planned to head straight for the industrial estate. If Rick was at the workshop, she could talk to him there and then. If not she'd wait.

But as she'd reached the sign pointing towards the estate, Sarah had lost her nerve. She had to tell Rick she knew the dog was stolen. She had to tell him that she'd been to see the owner. Somehow she needed to convince him that what he was doing was wrong. He had to take the dog back. Only, just at that moment, she didn't feel as though she had enough courage or the right words.

One thing was certain. She couldn't let Wolf ... Jack ... spend one more night in that dingy old building.

So instead of the industrial estate, she'd gone to the shopping centre. She sat down on the bench opposite the shoe shop. Gruff stood beside her, watching people pass by. Every now and then he lifted his head, his nose twitching as the smell of baking from the pasty shop drifted towards them.

Sarah didn't seem to notice it. She was too scared. Scared that Rick would lose his temper; scared for the dog. If Rick managed to find somewhere else to hide him without telling her, what could she do then? The poor animal needed her help just as much as the Dixons boy did.

She was so lost in her thoughts that she didn't see Rick marching towards her. It was only when Gruff started fidgeting and wagging his tail slightly that she spotted him. Gruff's greeting was a little cautious. He still didn't seem sure whether Rick was a friend or not.

Sarah's heart sank.

'You didn't come to the workshop this morning,' Rick said bluntly. 'I thought you would.' He glanced at Gruff. 'So we could walk the dogs.'

'I was going to,' Sarah answered, 'only then Josie came round early and I couldn't.'

'Well, let's go now.'

'And where are we going to take them, Rick?' she asked softly. 'There's nowhere, is there? Because you're so worried about being seen with … Wolf.'

Rick frowned. 'There are roads round the estate. Other roads not near the supermarket. We'll go there.'

Sarah said nothing.

Rick's frown deepened to a scowl. 'So, are you going to come with me, or what?'

She didn't want to. She'd have to tell him what she knew. He'd be furious.

'*Help me, God.*' The prayer ran silently through her head. '*I don't know how to do this. Please help me.*'

Sarah stood up. Gruff's tail started to wag more enthusiastically. Perhaps they were on the move at last.

'Let's go, then,' she said.

They walked to the workshop without talking. Both of them were keeping a wary eye out for anyone they might know. Topz could be out and about. Dixons had a way of creeping up. Neither Sarah nor Rick knew what they'd say if they were seen together again. Whatever explanation they came up with, it would still look odd.

As Rick slid back the workshop door, Wolf bounded forward. Gruff pulled Sarah inside excitedly, happy to see his new friend. Reaching across one of the workbenches, Rick grabbed his belt and looped it through Wolf's red collar. Then suddenly he stopped still and stared at Sarah full in the face.

'What?' he demanded. 'Something's up. What is it?'

Sarah couldn't look at him. Slowly, reluctantly, she reached into the pocket of her hoodie and pulled out a folded piece of paper.

Rick was watching her closely. He shook his head. 'What's that?'

She held it out. Rick took it. Keeping his eyes more on Sarah than on the paper, he unfolded it. But the moment he saw the photo of the dog with the name, Jack, underneath, the 'MISSING' poster had his full attention.

'Where did you get this?' he muttered.

'I saw one down at the park,' Sarah said quietly. 'There are a few on the lamp posts around Makepiece Avenue, too. But actually …' She gulped nervously. 'Actually, *Jack's* owner printed that one off and gave it to me.'

That's when she saw Rick's eyes flash. 'What do you mean, *Jack's owner?*' His gaze slid to the black dog by his side. 'What's this got to do with me?'

Sarah didn't answer.

Rick stared at her. 'Oh, I get it,' he nodded, spitting the words through clenched teeth. 'You think this is Jack, don't you? Well, it isn't. I told you, his name's Wolf. He's *mine*. He got given to me. I don't know who *this* dog is,' and he jabbed the photo with his finger, 'but it's not my Wolf.'

Sarah was trembling now, but she couldn't back off.

'I went to Number One, Makepiece Avenue, Rick,' she said as calmly as she could. 'I met Graham. He's really upset.'

'I don't know any Graham,' Rick snapped. He was looking more and more flustered, grinding his teeth together as Sarah spoke. 'And I don't know what you're talking about. *This*,' he hissed, thrusting the poster under Sarah's nose, 'has got nothing to do with me. It's a different dog! Can't you see that? **It doesn't even LOOK LIKE WOLF!'**

Sarah winced as Rick's voice rose to a yell.

'You shouldn't shout,' she said. 'Someone'll hear.'

Rick crumpled the poster in his hands and threw the

ball of paper into a corner of the workshop. His fingers started pulling nervously at his top lip.

'Graham thinks Jack escaped from his garden. He said the fence at the back was all broken down. He feels guilty, Rick,' Sarah muttered. 'He thinks it's his fault that Jack got out.'

'Stop calling him Jack!' Rick growled. 'His name's Wolf! He's not Jack, he's Wolf!'

Suddenly it hit him. If Sarah had been talking to Graham, what had she said? Had she given him away? He looked towards the door. For all he knew, Graham was on his way there already.

Rick took a step towards her, glaring. 'What did you tell him? You'd better not have said anything.'

'I didn't,' Sarah mumbled. 'I just said I was out walking Gruff a lot and I'd keep my eyes open for … Wolf …'

Just then, Wolf seemed to lose interest in Gruff and began to nuzzle Rick's knee. The Dixons boy watched him for a moment. Slowly, he hunched down, put his arms around him and buried his face in the dog's neck.

'You see?' he said. 'Wolf loves me. He's showing me he loves me, see? And I love him. That Graham doesn't. He doesn't care that he's gone, either. If he told you he did, then he's lying.'

'But you took him, Rick,' Sarah said gently. 'You stole his dog and that's wrong.'

'Well, what Graham was doing is wrong, too!'

There was silence. Then Rick turned his head to look at Sarah. To her amazement, she saw there were tears in his eyes.

'Graham left him outside,' he went on miserably. 'All the time. I don't think he ever took him for a walk. I know he hasn't lived there long, but every time I went past, Wolf was shut out in the back garden. You can't love a dog and then not bother with it,' he gulped. 'Just like you can't love a *person* and then leave them behind ...' He lifted a hand and wiped the back of it across his nose. 'I know what it looks like, Sarah, but I didn't steal Wolf. Really,' he said. 'I rescued him.'

Fifteen

Sarah sat on the grass near the skateboard park, knees tucked up under her chin. Gruff's lead was looped loosely round her wrist. He snuffled about, pricking up his ears every now and then when he heard voices; wagging his tail if he spotted another dog in the distance.

Sarah didn't want to go home. When she did, she knew she'd have to tell her mum about Wolf and she wasn't ready for that yet. For now she just wanted to be somewhere by herself with God. The skateboard park was empty. She was mostly hidden from the main path behind a tree. This spot on the grass was good.

*God, I need to talk to you about Rick. I need you to help me show him somehow **how much** You love him.*

The thing is – he doesn't feel loved by anybody. He thinks his dad doesn't want him. He thinks his mum cares more about his twin sisters.

He doesn't like the twins very much, God. If it hadn't been for them, he said his dad might have stayed. They were all right, just the three of them – Rick, his mum and his dad. But then the twins came along and he says that's when everything changed.

I told him it's not their fault. I said he shouldn't ever think it was his fault, either. I said sometimes things just happen with parents and they can't seem to get on with each other any more. And just because his dad's moved away now, I said, it doesn't mean he's stopped loving him either. It just means it's difficult for them to spend time together.

*But then Rick said that if his dad **hadn't** stopped loving him, maybe that was because he never loved him in the first place. 'How would I know if he did or not?' he said. 'He never told me. Ever.'*

After that, Rick talked about his birthday last year. He said that that was the day his dad moved away. He said he cried all night.

I don't know why he told me that, God. He's Rick from the Dixons Gang and he told me he cried! Topz'll never believe it. Not that I'll ever tell them. Not that part anyway. That's Rick's private stuff. It's not for me to talk about it with anyone else. He probably wishes he hadn't told me anyway.

*But, God, You already know all that, don't You? When he was crying, You saw him. You were there and it broke Your heart because he was so upset. Rick needs You **so much** God. He **needs** Your love. Not just me telling him about it, he needs to **feel** it properly for himself.*

Dixons laugh about Topz, I know they do. They think we're boring and we never do anything fun because we're always in church or having dull 'prayer meetings'. That's what they say when they tease us. But they don't understand what it's really like being friends with You. They have no idea how INCREDIBLE it is knowing that

You're beside us every single day.

*If Rick knew that, God, then I know his life would never be the same again. He'd know that he's not on his own. He'd know that You're always there to help him. He'd know that You'll never ever **ever** leave him.*

*It might take him a while to believe that – really and truly believe it – but he would in the end because it's true. That's Your promise to each one of us, isn't it, God, and You'll **never** break it.*

If Rick knew You, he'd know he was loved. And I know I'm going on a bit, and I will stop in a minute because I have to go home and talk to my mum. But I need to talk to You about Wolf quickly, too. You know what's happened with him. You know Rick has to give him back. Please, please help him to do that, God. Please, please let the right thing happen.

Sarah's eyes were wide open. She was staring straight ahead, but it was a moment before she noticed Josie and Dave. They'd spotted her behind the tree and crossed the grass to where she was sitting. Now, they stood looking down at her.

'Sarah?' Josie was frowning. 'What are you doing here? Are you all right?'

For a moment, Sarah was startled.

Then she shook her head slowly. 'No,' she answered. 'No, I'm not.'

Rick looked at his watch. It must have been well over an hour since Sarah had left. He hadn't moved from the workshop floor where he'd been cuddling Wolf. The black dog was now stretched out in front of him. As Rick sat there, he kept rubbing the palm of his hand backwards and forwards over the animal's upturned tummy.

'We'll be all right, you and me, Wolf,' Rick murmured. 'Sarah says I have to take you back, but I won't. That Graham doesn't love you. I don't know why he's sticking posters up about you because he doesn't want you back. Not really. Sarah doesn't understand that. I don't think she even believes me. But *we* know, don't we? We know what you've been through. That's why you're not going back.'

Rick fell silent, thinking. Where could he hide Wolf now? He wished so much Sarah had never seen him come to the workshop. She'd ruined *everything*. Wolf would have been safe there if it hadn't been for her. For a little while at least. Even if new people did start to rent the place from his dad, Rick could talk to them. They might not mind having a dog around. They might say that Wolf could still stay. Now he'd have to try and find somewhere else.

Slowly, he got to his feet. His legs felt stiff and cramped from being curled up on the floor for so long. He stretched. Wolf rolled over and got up, too. Giving himself a shake, he stood looking up at Rick expectantly.

The boy fished in his pocket and pulled out some coins. They made up the last of his money. He counted them quickly. There was just about enough for one more tin of dog food, he reckoned.

But then what? What about tomorrow? And the

next day? What was he going to give Wolf to eat then? He and the other two Dixons boys had pinched bags of crisps from shops before. Tins would be much harder. They were too bulky. Anyway, when he stole things with Dixons, it was all part of the games they played. Stupid dares. Stupid, dangerous ways to have a laugh.

This would be different. This would be deadly serious.

He shoved the coins back into his pocket, then cast his eyes miserably over Wolf. 'Some rescue this turned out to be, huh?' he said, stroking the dog's head.

The next few words were on Rick's lips so quickly he barely had time to realise what he was saying: *'God, help me, I don't know what to do ...'*

As he heard the prayer come out of his mouth, Rick looked almost surprised. He fingered the longer, thicker hair around the back of Wolf's neck. What was it Sarah had said ...? *'... even the hairs of your head have all been counted ...'*

Suddenly, his eyes grew wide. He sucked in his breath as a thought struck him. He turned it over in his mind.

What time was it? He glanced at his watch. The afternoon was racing by, but if he was quick, he might just make it.

He grabbed the plastic bag Sarah had brought full of Wolf's bedding, and thrust the cushions and blankets back inside. He emptied the water bowl in the sink and stuffed it in there, too. The ice cream carton he'd used for Wolf's food he'd throw in a litterbin on his way out of the industrial estate.

With his belt, looped through Wolf's collar, in one hand and the bag in the other, Rick stepped outside. It was getting colder now as the sun slipped lower in the sky. He dropped the bag and went to slide the door of the workshop closed. He paused for one moment, glancing around the inside to make sure he hadn't left anything. Then he rammed the door shut and turned the key in the lock.

Picking up the bag, he set off down the lane, the dog trotting along beside him. The Dixons boy was smiling. If Sarah went back there with Graham – or with anyone come to that – they wouldn't find a thing.

Wolf would be long gone.

Sixteen

Sarah, Josie and Dave stood uncertainly on the pavement outside Number One, Makepiece Avenue. They'd dropped Gruff back at Sarah's on the way.

None of them were quite sure what to say to Jack's owner, Graham. How to explain what had happened; why his dog was being looked after in a workshop on the industrial estate.

More than anything, what Sarah *didn't* want to do was get Rick into trouble. He'd done something bad, of course he had. But at the same time, just over a year ago his dad and his dog had gone away – left him. He'd just needed something to love. More importantly, he'd needed something to love him back.

Even before the three of them could walk through the still broken gateway, the front door to Number One opened.

'Hello, there,' Graham said. 'Spotted you from my window.' He looked at Sarah. 'You're the girl who came earlier, aren't you? Have you heard something? Have you seen Jack?'

Sarah glanced at Dave. He gave her a half-smile, but he didn't say anything. It was best that Sarah told Graham herself.

She took a step forward. 'Yes,' she began slowly. 'Yes, I have.'

Graham's eyes lit up. 'Where? Where is he?'

It didn't take Sarah long to explain once she got started. She told Graham about Rick. How much he loved dogs. How his family used to have one until his parents split up. How much he wanted another one; a dog of his very own, but his mum had said no.

Graham didn't interrupt. He listened intently.

It was when Sarah got to the part about why Rick said he'd taken Jack that his owner's face fell. Sarah thought Graham would be cross. She thought he'd say, 'How ridiculous! Of course I look after my dog.' She was waiting for him to call Rick a thief. To march indoors and phone the police.

But he didn't do any of those things.

He hung his head and looked sad. Then it was his turn to explain.

'Jack's not my dog. Not really,' he said quietly. 'He belongs to my mum. She's seventy-five now and was as fit as a flea. When my dad was alive, they both ran a small farm. After he died seven years ago, she decided to carry on with it. She had someone in to help her with the work, and she got Jack for a bit of extra company. But he's got a lot of collie in him, Jack has, and he turned out to be brilliant helping with the sheep. He loved it. He'd run and run on that farm. He's an outdoor dog. A working dog.' He paused.

'Anyway,' and there was a sigh in his voice, 'last year my mum had a bad fall. She broke her hip and damaged her back. She was going to be in hospital for quite a while and she asked me if I'd look after Jack. Well, I was only living in a flat then, and I'm not a great walker, but I couldn't say no, could I? I'm all my mum's got, you see, and she's all I've got really.

'But, the longer she was in hospital, the more the doctors could see that there was a lot more wrong with her than just a broken hip. She was getting forgetful. Only, a lot worse than forgetful.

'In the end, the doctors said she couldn't live on her

own any more. She needed proper care. She'd have to go into a special home where she could be looked after. The farm would have to be put up for sale. The animals had all been sold off by then anyway.

'So that just left Jack. "You will take care of him, won't you?" my mum said. Well, it wasn't easy in the flat. I had no garden. I'm out working a lot. But I couldn't let her down. That's why I moved here. Jack loved being outdoors at the farm. I thought he could live outdoors in the garden. I've got him a kennel, so he's got shelter if he wants it. I'll show you if you like. That just seemed the best thing to do.

'I'm not good with animals like my mum is,' Graham added. 'So, your friend – Rick, is it? – he's probably right. I haven't been looking after Jack the way I should. And since I thought he'd run off, I've been thinking that what I'm doing isn't fair. He maybe wouldn't have got out if he hadn't been bored or … lonely. I realised that I've been keeping Jack because my mum asked me to, not because I really wanted to. That's why I felt so terrible when I thought I'd lost him; why I stuck those posters up.

'I'd decided that if I ever got him back, it was time to see about getting him rehomed. He needs to be with someone who's got the time for him. Someone who'll really love him.'

'What about your mum?' Sarah said. 'Won't she be upset?'

Graham smiled at her. 'My mum,' he replied, 'would be far more upset to think that her Jack wasn't happy. I'll have a talk with her. I'm sure she'll understand in the end.'

Sarah nodded. 'I'm so sorry. I didn't know Rick had

just taken Jack to start with. It was only when I saw the posters.'

'You've got nothing to be sorry for,' Graham said. 'It's me,' and he poked a finger into his chest, 'I'm the one who should be sorry. I haven't done right by that dog. I mean, I'm not saying that what your friend did was right, either,' he added, 'but he meant well, I'll give him that.'

As Sarah looked back at Dave and Josie just inside the gateway, she couldn't help smiling. Not because Graham wasn't angry after all and Rick wasn't going to get into trouble – although, of course, she was pleased about that.

Sarah was smiling because of what Graham had said. He'd called Rick, from the Dixons Gang, her friend.

Rick got up early on Monday morning. It was the last day of the holidays. Tomorrow he had to go back to school.

He hated it there, but he had to admit that the start of this term would be different.

For a little while at least, he had something to look forward to.

After Sarah had finished talking to Graham, she had sprinted all the way to the industrial estate. She didn't take Dave and Josie. She needed to do this on her own.

When she got to the workshop, it was all locked up. She ran round the back. Standing on tiptoe, she stretched up to see if she could spy Jack through the windows. They were very dirty, inside and out. Even when she rubbed a spot clean on the outside it was difficult to see in.

But what she *did* manage to see was that everything was gone. Jack's bed, his water bowl, the ice cream carton. She was too late! Rick had disappeared taking Jack with him. And Sarah was sure he'd make certain she never found that beautiful, black dog ever again.

Miserably, she had walked back round to the front of the workshop and sunk down by the door.

That's where Rick found her only a few moments later.

'What are you doing here?' he demanded.

'Looking for you, of course,' she replied, scrambling to her feet. 'I thought you'd taken … Wolf … somewhere else. I thought I was never going to see him again.'

'You weren't supposed to,' Rick muttered. He looked down at the dog beside him, his belt still attached to his collar. 'And if you're thinking of bringing that Graham here, you can forget it. I know what to do now. I know what's best for Wolf. **He's never having him back.'**

'I'm not bringing Graham here,' Sarah said. 'I wanted to tell you that you were right. Graham hasn't been looking after Jack … well, Wolf … properly. At least, he hasn't been giving him what he needs. That's what Graham said. But it's not his fault exactly. It's complicated. Anyway, he's going to get Wolf rehomed. Somewhere where he'll be given lots of attention. Lots of walks. So, you see, Wolf's going to be all right. Graham's going to ask at the rescue centre if they'll help him find someone.'

Rick blinked. 'At the rescue centre?' He nodded slowly, taking it all in. 'Well, if he's going to ask the rescue centre for help, he'd better go when they're open. Because that's where I've just been and they were closed.'

Sarah stared at him, confused. 'What? Why have you just been to the rescue centre?' she murmured.

'I didn't know what else to do,' Rick said. 'I've just about run out of dog food. Wolf couldn't stay here because you knew where he was and I was sure you were going to tell Graham. It made sense. Anyway, it was you that gave me the idea. You told me that's where your cat came from. She's ended up with a pretty good home, so I thought maybe it was the best thing.'

Sarah was smiling now. She couldn't help it. She could hardly believe what she was hearing. Leaning over, she ruffled Wolf's ears.

'I'm so glad you came back,' she beamed, 'because I've got something else to tell you. I told Graham about you. Please don't worry, you're not in trouble or anything,' she added quickly. 'I explained it all to him and he's not cross. He knows you were only worried about Wolf. The thing is, Graham wants to keep him while a really good home is found. He wants a bit of time to make it up to him, I think. You know, for leaving him outside on his own such a lot. But he was wondering if, while Wolf's still here, *you'd* like to take him for his walks. I mean, you don't have to. I just thought … you might want to.'

Rick listened in silence to everything Sarah said. On the inside he was yelling with excitement. On the outside, his mouth had dropped open, but not a single sound came out.

So that Monday morning, before the start of term, Rick had decided to make the most of his last day of freedom. Graham had said he could take Wolf out all day long if he wanted to. And that's what Rick planned to do.

As soon as he was dressed, he made for his bedroom door. Just before he reached it, he stopped.

There were two things he hadn't done since the adventure with Wolf had started.

First, he hadn't said thank You to God. He didn't know why he wanted to thank Him exactly. Rick didn't often say thank you for anything. He wasn't even sure what had made him ask God for help in the first place when he'd never really spoken to Him before.

But he *had* asked and God had helped, so it seemed only right to say thank You.

God, I don't really know how to do this. I don't say prayers. Not normally. It's just that I asked You to help and I think You must have done. So I guess what I want to say is thank You. Wolf's going to be OK now. He won't have to be on his own all the time. He's going to get some good walks, too. I don't think I could have sorted that out on my own. Thanks for looking after him ... and me.

The second thing Rick hadn't done was open his birthday card. The one from his dad that he'd thrown behind his chest of drawers days ago. He'd mostly forgotten about it. But that morning, he suddenly remembered.

He carefully shifted the chest out from against the wall, put his hand in behind and pulled out the envelope. He sat on his bed for a moment, looking at it. Then, ripping it apart, he slid out the card. It had a picture of a motorbike on the front.

Rick went to open it and two folded twenty pound notes fell into his lap. There was a photo, too. It showed a short-haired, black and white dog; tongue hanging out, blue eyes bright. The other Wolf.

Rick's dad's writing was on the card:

Happy birthday, Rick.

I miss you, son.

I'm sorry I can't be with you any more, but I'll always love you.

Don't ever forget that.

Dad

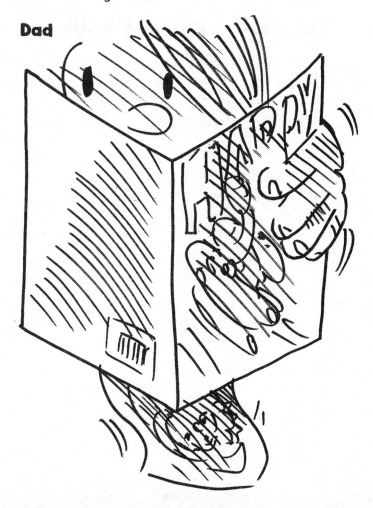

Just those few words in black biro.

Rick sat staring at them. He read them over several times; tried to hear his dad's voice.

He put the money and photo carefully in a drawer, and stood the card up on top of the chest.

At his bedroom door, he paused briefly to wipe the back of one hand over his eyes.

Then he went out.

His Wolf needed a walk.

NATIONAL DISTRIBUTORS

UK: (and countries not listed below)

CWR, Waverley Abbey House, Waverley Lane, Farnham, Surrey GU9 8EP.

Tel: (01252) 784700 Outside UK (44) 1252 784700 Email: mail@cwr.org.uk

AUSTRALIA: KI Entertainment, Unit 21 317-321 Woodpark Road, Smithfield, New South Wales 2164.

Tel: 1 800 850 777 Fax: 02 9604 3699 Email: sales@kientertainment.com.au

CANADA: David C Cook Distribution Canada, PO Box 98, 55 Woodslee Avenue, Paris, Ontario N3L 3E5.

Tel: 1800 263 2664 Email: sandi.swanson@davidccook.ca

GHANA: Challenge Enterprises of Ghana, PO Box 5723, Accra.

Tel: (021) 222437/223249 Fax: (021) 226227 Email: ceg@africaonline.com.gh

HONG KONG: Cross Communications Ltd, 1/F, 562A Nathan Road, Kowloon.

Tel: 2780 1188 Fax: 2770 6229 Email: cross@crosshk.com

INDIA: Crystal Communications, 10-3-18/4/1, East Marredpalli, Secunderabad – 500026, Andhra Pradesh.

Tel/Fax: (040) 27737145 Email: crystal_edwj@rediffmail.com

KENYA: Keswick Books and Gifts Ltd, PO Box 10242-00400, Nairobi.

Tel: (020) 2226047/312639 Email: sales.keswick@africaonline.co.ke

MALAYSIA: Canaanland, No. 25 Jalan PJU 1A/41B, NZX Commercial Centre, Ara Jaya, 47301 Petaling Jaya, Selangor.

Tel: (03) 7885 0540/1/2 Fax: (03) 7885 0545 Email: info@canaanland.com.my

Salvation Publishing & Distribution Sdn Bhd, 23 Jalan SS 2/64, 47300 Petaling Jaya, Selangor.

Tel: (03) 78766411/78766797 Fax: (03) 78757066/78756360 Email: info@salvationbookcentre.com

NEW ZEALAND: KI Entertainment, Unit 21 317-321 Woodpark Road, Smithfield, New South Wales 2164, Australia.

Tel: 0 800 850 777 Fax: +612 9604 3699 Email: sales@kientertainment.com.au

NIGERIA: FBFM, Helen Baugh House, 96 St Finbarr's College Road, Akoka, Lagos.

Tel: (01) 7747429/4700218/825775/827264 Email: fbfm_1@yahoo.com

PHILIPPINES: OMF Literature Inc, 776 Boni Avenue, Mandaluyong City.

Tel: (02) 531 2183 Fax: (02) 531 1960 Email: gloadlaon@omflit.com

SINGAPORE: Alby Commercial Enterprises Pte Ltd, 95 Kallang Avenue #04-00, AIS Industrial Building, 339420.

Tel: (65) 629 27238 Fax: (65) 629 27235 Email: marketing@alby.com.sg

SOUTH AFRICA: Struik Christian Books, 80 MacKenzie Street, PO Box 1144, Cape Town 8000.

Tel: (021) 462 4360 Fax: (021) 461 3612 Email: info@struikchristianmedia.co.za

SRI LANKA: Christombu Publications(Pvt)Ltd, Bartleet House, 65 Braybrooke Place, Colombo 2.

Tel: (9411) 2421073/2447665 Email: dhanad@bartleet.com

USA: David C Cook Distribution Canada, PO Box 98, 55 Woodslee Avenue, Paris, Ontario N3L 3E5, Canada.

Tel: 1800 263 2664 Email: sandi.swanson@davidccook.ca

Topz is a colourful daily devotional for 7- to 11-year-olds.

In each issue the Topz Gang teach children biblical truths through word games, puzzles, riddles, cartoons, competitions, simple prayers and daily Bible readings.

Available as an annual subscription
£15.50 (6 bimonthly issues includes p&p)
or as single issues **£2.85**.

Go to **www.cwr.org.uk/store**,
call 01252 784700 or visit a Christian bookshop.

Prices correct at time of printing.

You'll also love
Topz Secret Diaries

Alexa Tewkesbury's *Topz Secret Diaries* hit the balance between humour and insightful truth as they bring well-loved Topz characters to life.

Benny's Barmy Bits
ISBN: 978-1-85345-431-8

Danny's Daring Days
ISBN: 978-1-85345-502-5

Dave's Dizzy Doodles
ISBN: 978-1-85345-552-0

**Gruff & Saucy's
Topzy-Turvy Tales**
ISBN: 978-1-85345-553-7

John's Jam-Packed Jottings
ISBN: 978-1-85345-503-2

Josie's Jazzy Journal
ISBN: 978-1-85345-457-8

Paul's Potty Pages
ISBN: 978-1-85345-456-1

Sarah's Secret Scribblings
ISBN: 978-1-85345-432-5

Go to **www.cwr.org.uk/store**,
call 01252 784700 or visit a Christian bookshop.

Boys Only and Just for Girls

These special editions of *Topz Secret Diaries* will help you
discover things about yourself and God with questions and
quizzes, engaging puzzles, word searches, doodles,
lists to write and more.

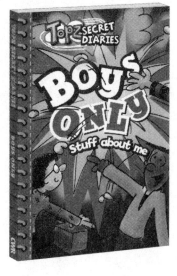

Topz Secret Diaries: Boys Only
ISBN: 978-1-85345-596-4

Topz Secret Diaries: Just for Girls
ISBN: 978-1-85345-597-1

126-page paperbacks, 129x197mm

Go to www.cwr.org.uk/store,
call 01252 784700 or visit a Christian bookshop.